1

Vacationing In A Combat Zone

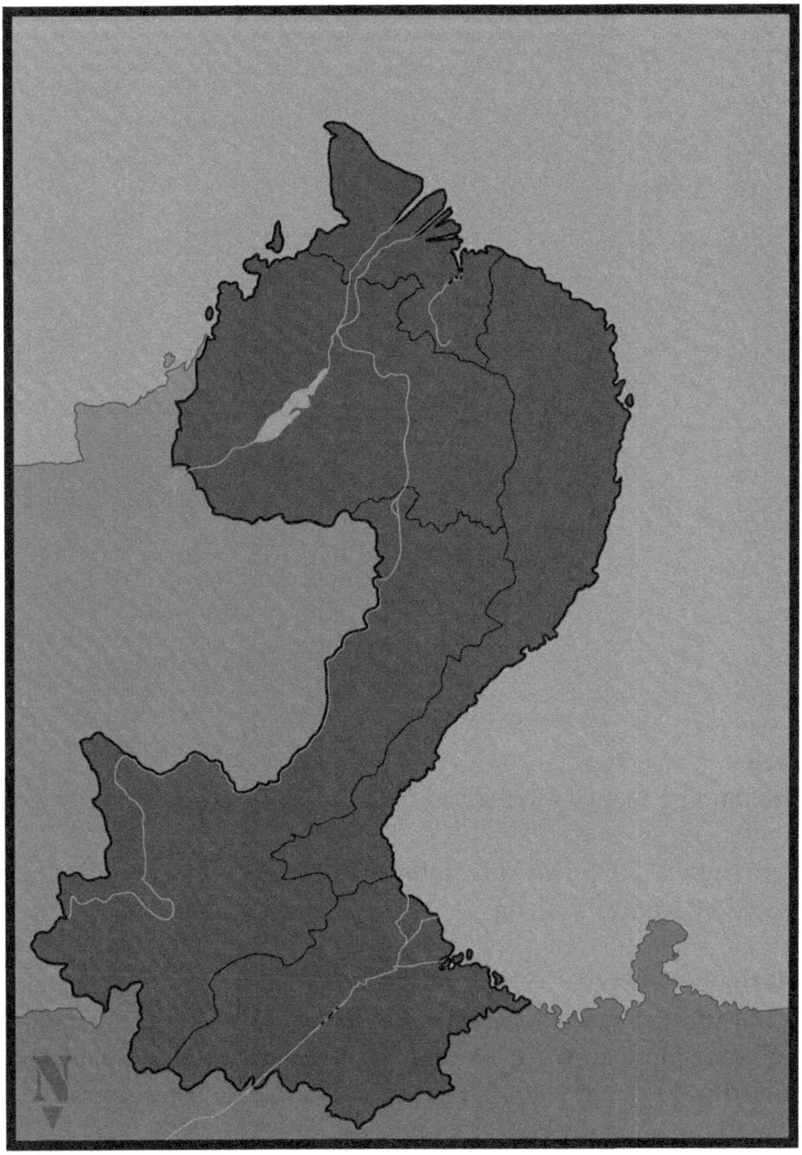

A Novel by David L. Johnson

R&R
Vacationing in a Combat Zone

Copyright © 2025 David L. Johnson's Estate and Martin R. Carlson
Edited by Martin Carlson

All rights reserved. No part of this publication may be reproduced or transmitted in any form whatsoever, electronic or mechanical, including photocopying, recording, or by any informational storage or retrieval system without express written, dated and signed permission from the copyright holder.

ISBN: 978-1-326-55843-7
Imprint: Lulu.com

Table of Contents

Chapter 1   The Mission
Chapter 2   The Journey
Chapter 3   Fear And Loathing
Chapter 4   Yard To The Rescue
Chapter 5   The Bell Tolls
Chapter 6   The Cav and The Alamo
Chapter 7   Cavalry To The Rescue
Chapter 8   Shangri-La
Chapter 9   Of Ravens And Bad Ammo
Chapter 10   Ancient Tribes
Chapter 11   Jolly Green T-Rex
Chapter 12   Beer, Steaks, And A Ten Thousand Dollar Question
Chapter 13   Thousand Yard Stare Or Gratefully Dead
Chapter 14   Short Timers
Chapter 15   Damage Done
Chapter 16   Three Escape The Cav
Chapter 17   The Yellow Brick Road
Chapter 18   Americanization
Chapter 19   Bad Troop's Pay
Chapter 20   Creative Funding
Chapter 21   Khe Sanh
Chapter 22   Big LZ
Chapter 23   No Honeymoon
Chapter 24   Friendly Fire
Chapter 25   Blast From The Past
Chapter 26   A Company Job
Chapter 27   R And R

CHAPTER 1
The Mission

Doc set out for the club with a grim look of determination on his face. He'd seen a lot of his friends die and needed to do what he could do to find out why. Now, today, he had been presented with an opportunity to do just that.

It was 1970 and the Army had just taken over Dong Ha combat base from the Marines, who were in the process of leaving Vietnam. The enlisted men's club wasn't much to look at, just plywood walls and floor, with a corrugated tin roof to keep out the monsoon rains. Like all the other buildings on the base it was surrounded by a three foot high sandbag wall to protect its occupants from enemy rockets and mortars. The only thing to distinguish it from the other buildings, or hootches as the men called them, was a pair of swinging saloon style doors. Doc walked into the club in a trance. His mind was wandering somewhere up on the Plain of Jars in Laos.

The sound of a loud bell ringing in his ears brought him back to reality. He had mistakenly walked into the club with his boonie hat still on.

There was a rule at the club printed in large black letters above the bar which stated, "Any soldier entering this club with his hat on will buy a round for the house." Luckily there were only about twenty men in the club at the time and at ten cents a beer Doc could afford the two dollars even on military pay. Everyone in the club quickly ran up to the bar for their free beer. Doc received a great number of slaps on the back and thank-yous from his new found friends. He paid the bartender, took a sip of beer and thought to himself about what a poor start this was to his mission. Doc just hoped it wasn't an

omen of things to come.

He heard someone call from a table behind him. "Hay Doc, you ain't never gonna get rich that way." Doc turned around and there was Cyrano sitting at a table with a couple of rather together looking dudes in camouflage fatigues he'd never seen before. It was obvious these guys were not from the Cavalry and not just because they wore those strange looking tiger stripe uniforms.

Doc sat down at the table and was introduced to Fingers and The Monkey Man. They were Special Forces and were working on some sort of a business deal with Cyrano. Doc shook hands with the newcomers. One of them, Fingers, who like all Green Berets had received army medical training said, "Always good to meet a fellow medic with some combat experience. We could use a guy like you."

"Where the hell are you guys from?" Doc said.

Fingers answered, "The Great Northwest. If you want to see the place just tag along with Cyrano here tomorrow morning. It might give you a chance to see what's really going on in this crazy part of the world. It just might turn out to be a lot bigger than you think it is."

"This is perfect timing," Doc said, "my R and R starts tomorrow and I know damn well those Australian kangaroos aren't going to tell me what I want to know."

"I like your attitude," said Fingers, as he raised his beer can as if in a toast to this new member of the unit.

They all clicked their beer cans together as a sort of understood agreement, and proceeded to get very drunk.

It was a good time. They sat around the club telling war stories for several hours. Doc was having trouble keeping up with the way these guys were drinking. Cyrano noticed Doc weaving on the way back from the bar with four beers so he talked one of the Special Forces boys into giving him a little something to keep him going. The Monkey Man handed Doc a handful of capsules saying "Army issue speed guaranteed to keep you going. In half an hour you *will* be sober whether you like it or not."

Doc took two of them not really believing they'd work. Thirty minutes later though he felt like a new man and was starting to out talk everybody at the table. "It looks like we've created a monster," Fingers said to the Monkey Man. "Doc if you don't pipe down I'm gonna have to start force feeding you beer just to slow you down." Fingers looked like he meant it. So with a great deal of effort Doc managed to keep his comments to a minimum. It wasn't easy with that so called army issue speed coursing through his veins.

Fingers turned to Cyrano and said, "Now don't you guys forget we meet at the Rock Pile Firebase at ten hundred hours tomorrow morning, and don't forget the whores."

"No problem," said Cyrano, "It's all taken care of, I just want to get a chance to check out those prehistoric jars I've been hearing about up on that plain in your AO (area of operation). I don't know if it's true or not but according to some of the mountain people I've talked to they're filled with gold."

"I've never heard of any prehistoric jars," said Fingers, "but if they're there our people will find them."

"You know," said The Monkey Man, "we were told when we arrived at the Plain de Jars that the French named it because of the jar shaped mountains surrounding the place."

Doc had been listening to this conversation without saying a word for some time, but he couldn't keep his mouth shut any longer. "They're trying to keep it a secret," he said. "Those jars must be so valuable they don't want anyone to know they even exist."

"There it is!" Said Cyrano.

"Doc you finally said something that makes sense." Said Fingers, "This is beginning to sound interesting. We are definitely going to have to do some investigating into this here jar thing. The only problem is the plain is usually a hot area. It's the traditional battle ground for all the tribes surrounding it. I've even heard stories about China and Japan fighting major battles there during World War Two. Now it's supposed to be used by the NVA as part of their Ho Chi Min Trail, even though it's a long way to the west from Vietnam."

"Which reminds me of the main reason we're here," said The Monkey Man. "Within an hour we've got to appropriate ourselves a helicopter and fly it to the Rock Pile Firebase so we can meet you guys and those three women you promised us tomorrow morning. Right Cyrano?"

"Right on Monkey Man, we'll be there."

Just then a very large and very drunk soldier came staggering by spilling beer all over the table. Fingers was on him instantly with "I suggest you clean up that table right now while you're still capable of it!"

The drunk tanker looked at him indignantly. "A little guy like you ain't goin' to tell me what to do just because he wears one of those special faggot uniforms."

The Monkey Man looked at Fingers and said, "I told you this would happen if we came in to this shit house club." With that they both stood up, pulled their green berets from their pockets, and with a slow and deliberate motion put them on their heads. This time the bell did not ring.

The large drunk tanker threw a roundhouse punch at Fingers, he caught the man's arm in midair and used the momentum to flip him through the air with what looked like some sort of a judo throw. The man landed on the next table which buckled under his weight and crashed to the floor.

That's when all hell broke loose. The big guy's buddies rushed the two waiting Green Berets like a pack of wild dogs. There were bodies flying everywhere. It looked just like one of those old time cowboy movies.

In the confusion of the melee Cyrano and Doc managed to sneak to the door without being attacked or even noticed. As they watched from a safe distance the overwhelming odds were starting to get the best of Fingers and The Monkey Man. The Monkey Man was on the floor and about to be wasted from a heel stomp when Fingers reached into the side pocket of his tiger striped pants and pulled a forty-five out of a specially designed leg holster. He quickly fired two shots into the ceiling, freezing everyone in their tracks. He slowly bent down, while still keeping his eyes on the crowd he grabbed The Monkey Man by the shoulder and helped him up. The Monkey Man dusted himself off and said, "You wasted a bullet, one would have been sufficient. You know how hard it is to get forty-five rounds since these damn tankers got here with those damn grease guns (machine guns issued to tankers that fired 45 rounds.)

"Sorry, I got excited, let's dee-dee," said Fingers. Doc and Cyrano had snuck out the door and were waiting there. Fingers and The Monkey Man slowly backed out the door still holding the crowd at gun point.

As they slid out the door The Monkey Man saw Cyrano and said, "Key." Cyrano handed him a key and The Monkey Man whispered to Cyrano "Charlie Mike ten hundred hours, Rock Pile."

Charlie Mike is military radio code for continue mission. Each letter in the alphabet has its own word: A-Alpha, B-Bravo, C-Charlie, etc. The Monkey Man told Cyrano to continue mission, or meet him at the Rock Pile at 10:00 AM.

With that they were off running in the direction of the officers quarters and Headquarters area. "We better get out of here." Doc said.

"Yea," said Cyrano, "up to the bunker, but be cool, we don't want to run and draw any attention."

They walked as casually as possible towards the bunker and just got around the corner of the bar when they heard the old west styled saloon swinging bar doors slowly swing open, followed by a hoarse scream of "There they go." All of a sudden what must have been the entire crowd inside the bar went rushing through the bar doors, knocking them both off their hinges.

The drunk and screaming mob took off running in the direction of HQ where Doc could see Fingers and The Monkey Man disappear behind a building. A few minutes later Doc and Cyrano were just about at the bunker when they heard the colonels chopper start up. They climbed to the top of the bunker, one of the highest spots on the base and watched the chopper warming up, its engine quickly getting louder and then the prop blades beginning to spin. They could also see the guys from the Enlisted Men's Club. The tankers had somehow managed to run right by Fingers and The Monkey Man, and were spreading out searching behind every pile of sandbags and under every hootch they saw. At first they didn't think anything of the chopper starting up. Not until it attempted to lift off the ground. Attempted was the word for it. They managed to get a couple of feet off the ground and then bounced right back down again.

One of the tankers finally noticed the floundering chopper and yelled to the rest, "That's got to be them." The whole group then took off running towards the Green Berets who were desperately trying to get the chopper off the ground.

The Monkey Man who was laboring to fly the thing finally realized what was wrong. "The key you dumb shit, you forgot to unlock the chain" he yelled to Fingers.

The colonel had had this problem before and since military vehicles didn't come with ignition keys, he'd ordered chains and padlocks for them.

Fingers quickly jumped out the open door and unlocked the padlock. He heard someone yell from a distance, "Get those Airborne mother fuckers." He looked up and saw the gang of tankers running straight at him from just a hundred yards away. He jumped back in, looked at The Monkey Man, pointed straight up and yelled, "Sky" at the top of his lungs.

The chopper lifted off the ground just as the angry tankers got to it. One of them managed to jump up and grab the skids with both hands. The weight was enough to slow the choppers ascent. It started listing to the right and looked liked it was going to crash. The Monkey Man desperately fought with the controls trying to stabilize the chopper while Fingers leaned out the door and stomped on the tankers hands until he let go and fell the short distance to the ground. The chopper wobbled hard from the sudden loss of weight. Fingers barely managed to keep his balance and then crawled back in as the chopper slowly began to stabilize. "I thought you said you could fly one of these things?" He said.

"I took a two hour course on it at Fort Holabird, it was a good course but we had one small problem."

"What was that?" Said Fingers.

"They didn't have any choppers there to practice in."

"You mean you've never really flown one before?"

"Don't worry," said The Monkey Man, "I learn fast."

With that the chopper lurched forward slowly gaining speed, but unfortunately without enough height to miss the colonel's personal shitter. The chopper hit with one of the skids, knocking it over and swinging the chopper back in the opposite direction. Then it lurched forward again slowly gaining speed and height.

Cyrano and Doc were still watching from their vantage point on top the bunker. It was a very impressive show, but they'd had their doubts that Fingers and Monkey Man would make. They watched Fingers wave good-bye to the tankers. He yelled something to them but from where they were they couldn't hear what he said over the roar of the chopper.

Doc figured they had it made until he realized the chopper was headed directly at them. Cyrano and Doc looked at each other, then back at the chopper. Its direction did not change. At the last second they both dove off the bunker and hit the ground waiting in anticipation of the crash. Instead they heard the chopper fly right over them. Doc looked up just in time to see Fingers wave, and heard him cry out "Yee haa!" as they flew out over the perimeter, the circle of small sandbag bunkers with rolls of constantine or barbed wire loosely uncoiled between them.

"God damn cowboys'." Said Cyrano as the chopper flew off into the sunset headed west to the Rock Pile.

Even farther west from there was a mysterious land of mountains. The Monkey Man called it the Great Northwest Territory. The modern world calls it Laos. No one knows how many ancient names the land has been known by.

Chapter 2
THE JOURNEY

Cyrano and Doc stood up and brushed themselves off. They looked at each other and laughed, then Cyrano said "We did it Doc, we got ourselves a ride. A ride to the ancient land of Siam."

"Siam?" Said Doc.

"Ya, that's what Laos was called hundreds of years ago. It was supposed to be some sort of a mystical kingdom."

"Mystical?"

"Ya, Mystical, they were very rich. They had even more gold than Alexander the Great. I know there has got to be some of it left there, and I can't think of a better place to look than those jars up on the plain."

"Money's nice" said, Doc, "but I want to know the real reason we're here. Politics is nice too but I don't think its worth fighting wars over."

"I don't know," said Cyrano "but I've got a feeling that maybe we're better off not knowing."

"That might be true, but we're going to find out anyway. Looks like Fingers and The Monkey Man are right in the middle of it."

"Enough said for now, the future will tell" said Cyrano. "I do believe it's party time!"

They went straight through the night partying with the boys. That army issue speed was very potent. Doc couldn't have slept if he'd wanted to. He gave a few tablets of the stuff to Cyrano to keep him going too.

Back at the chopper pad the Colonel was slow to react to all the commotion going on out side his air-conditioned hootch. He'd been distracted by a young Vietnamese woman who was in bed with him. She was one of Cyrano's girls, the same one who had stolen the chopper key for him.

He quickly put on his olive drab underwear and ran outside just in time to see his chopper flying off into the sunset. After several red faced curses he ran back inside and told his radio man to call Quang Tri and tell them to send some choppers out to find his stolen bird.

Unfortunately for the Colonel the Airborne Rangers had a big operation going on and all of Quang Tri's choppers were in use.

Around four o'clock in the morning Doc and Cyrano decided it was time to start packing. Cyrano had his jeep locked up at the bunker. They left it there, out of sight from the rest of the base, so as not to attract any attention.

They walked the short distance to the medics' hootch. Then quietly packed what they thought they'd need into their water-proof bags. Doc made sure his medical bag was well supplied and threw that in too, hoping he wouldn't have to use it.

Cyrano had a canvas duffel bag under his cot filled with what he said would be all the weapons they'd need, two M-16s one M-79 grenade launcher and two 45s, plus enough ammunition to "hold off a Chinese human wave attack." The thing must have weighed a ton. It took both of them to carry it back to the jeep. He also had three cases of C-rations which he said were for trading purposes rather than for actual eating.

They were all loaded and ready to go well before the sun came up. The few clouds in the eastern sky were just beginning to glow pink and purple as the sun rose out of the South China Sea. It was a beautiful sight as they headed for their first stop in Quang Tri.

They stopped at the gate and chatted with the guard for a few minutes. They both knew the man so there were no questions asked about all the gear in the back. Doc told him they were headed out on R and R in Thailand. It was close to the truth since Thailand and Laos shared the same border. Besides Doc really was on his R and R. He was also beginning to have some doubts about his sanity.

The guard yelled out "get some for me." As they waved good-bye to Dong Ha and headed south down Highway 1 on their way to the village of Quang Tri. It was there that they were to pick up three of Cyrano's business partners. According to him they were the three best looking whores in all of South East Asia. Cyrano had a tendency to exaggerate at times but Doc did have to admit that Cyrano had damn good taste when it came to women.

That gorgeous sunrise was coming up to their left and as beautiful as it was, the blinding brilliance of it was beginning to remind Doc of the fact that he hadn't had any sleep yet.

Cyrano was feeling the same way. He lit up a joint and passed it to Doc saying "this should round off some of those edges. By the way I figure we should do a few more of those Green Beret pills before we start to crash. They should keep us awake until we get to the Rock Pile. When we get there well be able to get a nap."

Doc reached into his shirt pocket and pulled out his little plastic ear plug container, where he had stashed the speed. He'd lost the ear plugs months ago but the empty container worked well as a pill box, since it had a screw-on top and was water proof. Doc handed him a couple of the pills, "Where are we going to nap at the Rock Pile without either being killed or captured? As far as I know there aren't any secure areas anywhere near that place."

"We'll meet Fingers and The Monkey Man at the Rock Pile Fire Base, not out in the middle of nowhere." Replied Cyrano.

"Rock Pile Fire Base?"

"Yea, didn't you know we have a fire base there?"

"No. We cruised all over that place and I never saw it."

"It's well concealed on a mountain top surrounded by jungle." Explained Cyrano.

"I'll be damned." Said Doc. "I'm learnin' new things already."

"There ya are. As a matter of fact it was the Rock Pile Firebase that saved your ass from the Chinese at Lao Bao."

"I'm not sure being shelled by my own artillery counts as saving my ass, but I guess I'm still alive."

"There ya are." Said Cyrano as he swallowed the pills. "Ya know I've heard that if you take enough of these things you actually turn into a Green Beret." They both laughed as they headed down the Red Ball to Quang Tri.

CHAPTER 3
FEAR AND LOATHING

    The Monkey Man had pretty much mastered the art of flying a helicopter by the time they arrived at the Rock Pile Firebase. He was a good friend of the Commanding Officer there, Colonel Travis, who was already in on their little operation to steal the chopper. Colonel Travis and the Dong Ha Colonel were old enemies and besides Fingers had turned him on to a couple bottles of Jack Daniels as payment for a place to hide the chopper. Fingers and The Monkey Man finished the night with a small private party in the only air-conditioned room at the Rock Pile Firebase.

    Early the next morning Cyrano and Doc pulled into the village of Quang Tri. They parked the jeep in front of a typical looking Vietnamese hootch, an old Vietnamese woman came out the door when she heard the jeep pull up. She yelled out "Cyrano you come back to make me rich?"

"That's right Mama San. I need three girls this time, the three most beautiful girls you have."

"No sweat Cyrano, they already up and waiting for you."

"Great, let's get the show on the road."

Mama San went back in and came out a few seconds later with three of the best looking Vietnamese girls Doc had ever seen. They all looked as though they might have some French blood in them.

As they approached the jeep Doc noticed one of them looked familiar. Then he realized she was the VC sympathizer they'd choppered out from Mai Loc not more than two weeks earlier.

"Well, well, we meet again." Said Doc.

"Ah, I remember you," she said, "you the tank doctor."

Doc took her hand and helped her into the back of the jeep. "How did you get away from the ARVN interrogators?"

"No sweat, Mama San pay money to get me out and give me job. Very good job."

"I'll be damned, so that's the way things work here."

"There it fuckin' is" said Cyrano. "That's the way things work in the real world. So you two have already met?"

"We choppered her out of Mai Loc as a VC sympathizer on our last trip to the Rock Pile" said Doc.

"Oh shit," Said Cyrano. "You mean she's from the same area we're headed for?"

"Yea, I guess so."

"This is not a good situation but there's nothing I can do about it now. They're the only three she has and I promised The Monkey Man we'd bring three."

Doc and Cyrano pulled out of the village of Quang Tri and headed back up Highway 1 to the north in one very loaded down jeep. It was a strange sight even among the many strange sights of

Vietnam. Three teen-aged girls laughing and giggling in the back seat and two teen-aged boys looking somewhere between serious and ridiculous in the front.

They passed by Dong Ha without even slowing down. They were afraid some MP's might see them and pull them over. Since they were legally on R and R they weren't AWOL but they figured the MP's could have got them for something, although just what they weren't sure. At any rate they made it through without being noticed by any Americans.

When they got a ways past the village of Dong Ha, Doc said to Cyrano, "I think it's time to break out the weapons."

"Yea," said Cyrano "we're almost in Indian country now. By the way is Tray's boyfriend still alive?"

"He was when we left the Rock Pile. As a matter of fact he set up a booby trap for us when we scared them away from their camp. We almost caught them. We came so close that they had to leave most of their gear. We found a note book of his with Trays picture in it, his name is Hoang."

"Shit, this does not look good, if he sees us coming with her we could be in deep shit."

"Yea, I know, lock load and pray," said Doc.

They came to Highway 9 and took a left turn heading for the Rock Pile. "At least going this way we won't have to go through Mai Loc, their home village."

"I'd be willing to bet he's in the mountains anyway" Doc said. Then he turned to Tray, "Do you think your boyfriend is trying to find you?"

She gave Doc a very sad look and said, "Not know."
Doc then turned to Cyrano and said, "I sure as hell hope that kid doesn't see us coming,"

"Then again this just might work to our advantage" said Cyrano.

"I don't think he'll try to ambush us as long as we have her along, not unless he's pissed off at her enough to kill her."

"I hope you're right Cyrano."

"Yea, me too!"

A short while later they were starting the steep and winding uphill climb to the Rock Pile. The memories of the last two times Doc had taken this road came back to him. His heart beat increased ever so slightly as these memories flashed across his mind, gripping his M16 tighter yet knowing full well that if something really did happen it would be of little use. Cyrano was right, the best protection was the woman. Cyrano down shifted and gunned the engine. He drove as fast as he could around the steep and winding road. It was dangerous. If he were to lose control it would mean death for everyone in the Jeep. The shear cliffs along the sides of the road were so steep that there might be as much as a ten second drop to think about it before they plunged to the bottom of the ravine.

Doc noticed once again, to his horror, the large number of American vehicles that had taken that plunge in the past. The girls in the back seat had suddenly stopped their giggling and were now holding on to each other for dear life. Their already large eyes opened even wider with fear.

Cyrano knew it was dangerous to drive the way he was, but he also knew it was the safest way to make the climb. If Tray's boyfriend was up there he would know that an ambush, or even one well placed sniper round, would mean certain death for her.

"Hey Cyrano" said Doc, "what if there's a mine planted somewhere in this road?"

"If we hit a mine in this little jeep we'll all be dead no matter what speed we're travelin' at."

"Good point" said Doc.

Watching up above not far away was Hoang. He was with his two new cell members. The VC worked in groups of three called cells. They were always short of men, short of food and short of ammunition. This was a lucky day for them though, like the night he had attacked Doc's Cavalry platoon, they had just been given a great and magical weapon, a Russian RPG, a Rocket Propelled Grenade.

They had seen the fast moving dust cloud coming up the mountain from far off and had had plenty of time to hide behind a large bolder close to the road. Hoang sighted his new weapon in on a spot in the road where he knew the fast moving jeep would be passing, and waited. In just a few minutes he could hear the engine of the jeep growing very loud. He saw it come around a sharp bend in the road. The jeep was moving so fast it actually went up on two wheels for just a fraction of a second.

Because of the high speed he knew it would be a difficult shot. Hoang peered at the jeep through the sight of the RPG and waited for it to come to the spot. It would be very soon. He followed the movement of the jeep with his whole body as he had been taught by the Russian advisor and slowly started to squeeze the trigger. It was then that he recognized one of the three women in the back seat of the jeep. It was Tray. He loosened his grip on the trigger just in the nick of time. The jeep flew by, careened around another corner and went quickly out of sight again.

Hoang felt a deep rage slowly building within him. This was not right. The Americans had gone too far. His course of action was set. There was no choice in the matter. He had to get her back or die trying. Death he realized would be the most likely outcome of his actions. Death for many Americans yes, but his own death would be most likely. He knew this as a certainty, but his own death did not matter anymore, this was more important than his own life.

Hoang looked at his two friends, his eyes were beginning to tear, and hoarsely whispered "Tray". His friends knew Hoang would not miss the shot he had practiced so often, and now their confused looks cleared. Hoang pointed up the mountain and began to run as fast as he could, carrying the heavy Russian made RPG on his shoulder. His friends followed close behind.

He stood at the top of the mountain breathing heavily, watching the American jeep head off into the distance. He knew where they were headed, they all knew. The Americans could not survive alone in these mountains and there was only one of their bases anywhere close by. They knew the place well, the Americans called it the Rock Pile.

Cyrano and Doc made it to the Rock Pile Firebase with ten minutes to spare. It was o-nine fifty hours as they pulled into the base, but there was no sign of Fingers or The Monkey Man. After a short search though they did find the helicopter covered in camouflage netting.

Cyrano heard a friendly voice, "Hey Cyrano, what brings you up this way and who are these three lovely creatures you brought to our humble abode?"

"Taco old man, how ya doin'?" Cyrano answered, "long time no see. Hey man you seen the two Green Beret dudes that came in on that bird."

"They headed for the CO's hootch after they landed last night."

"Thanks Taco," replied Cyrano, "later man." They drove the jeep the short distance to the CO's hootch and stopped just outside the door.

Doc turned to Cyrano and said "What's the deal here? I thought these guys were supposed to have their shit together."

"Yea well I guess we're gonna' have to wake 'em up" said Cyrano as he climbed out of the jeep. He stretched for a few seconds, stiff from the long ride and then walked slowly to the door. He knocked a few times and waited.

The Monkey Man opened the door and motioned for them all to come in. It was obvious he'd just woken up. His eyes were glowing red and he had a tough time keeping his balance. He looked at his watch and said "Jeese, I was beginning to wonder if you guys were ever gonna' make it."

"No problem" said Cyrano."

Fingers staggered over and said "All right, you guys made it. Well done, damn outstanding. I wasn't sure you could really pull it off."

"Well guys, let's get down to business here", said The Monkey Man. "The Colonel of this here fire base is still sacked out in his room but he gave us permission to use a few of his back rooms here, so let's get to work."

Doc and Cyrano set up each of the girls in one of the small rooms while Fingers and The Monkey Man went around the base soliciting customers. It was an easy job. This was an extremely secluded outpost just on the edge of nowhere, and most of these men hadn't seen a woman in many moons. Within thirty minutes there were long lines formed at each of the doors to the rooms.

Doc and Cyrano had accomplished the first part of their mission and were able to relax for a while. They found a couple of unused cots and fell immediately into very deep and much needed sleep.

Chapter 4
YARD TO THE RESCUE

On another mountain top within sight of the Rock Pile Firebase, Hoang and his two friends began to make plans for the liberation of his lover. The use of force was completely out of the question since there were only three of them. Even if they had a whole battalion it would be doubtful if they could overrun the heavily armed Americans who could radio in helicopter and jet fighter support. Their only chance was to somehow sneak into the fire base undetected, find Tray and sneak back out.

It had to be done during the day because the two Americans would most likely leave before nightfall.

Their best chance would be a well planned ambush as the Americans were making their way back down the winding mountain road from the base. They could block off the road and when the jeep stopped they could pick off the Americans with sniper fire. This would be the best way to get her back safely. By then though it would be too late, the Americans would already have used her. No he could not let them get away with this. Hoang would have to somehow get her out before then.

An idea finally came to him. He knew the Americans worked with both the Montagnards, a member of a Vietnamese hill tribe, and the South Vietnamese army. Hoang was part Montagnard himself, which had been the cause of much shame throughout most of his life. For once this might work to his advantage.

He would get rid of anything that made him look like a VC and try to look as much as possible like a Montagnard soldier. Of course even this would not give him a reason to be walking into an American base where he didn't know anyone. He had to have a reason for coming into the base. He had to somehow need the Americans' help and still be able to keep his weapons.

There was only one thing that would work. He had to be wounded bad enough to need their help. Hoang knew what had to be done, and that it had to be done before telling his friends, because he knew they would try to talk him out of it.

He took the American make forty five out of his holster and looked at it for a moment. He was very proud of it, he had captured it himself two years earlier from a small platoon of Americans that he had helped ambush near his home village.

They were the same Americans who had killed his father just two days before. He had been out working in the rice fields at the time when he heard the automatic weapons fire coming from his village. He threw down his plow and ran as fast as he could to his father's house, where he saw the Americans walking away in the opposite direction.

His father's hootch was on fire, and his mother and sister were watching it burn in a state of shock. Hoang ran into the burning hootch and found his father's body, motionless on the dirt floor with a bullet hole in his head. Hoang quickly went to the trap door in the floor where his father kept the rifle he had used against the Japanese during World War Two many years ago

Although his father didn't like the idea of having more foreigners in his country he did not dislike the Americans. He had studied their form of government and believed their form of democracy was the best way to rule a country. He did not like communism because even though it was supposed to be for the people, he had seen that in actual practice it always became a dictatorship. He had seen this happen to his fellow countrymen in the north. They had defeated the French in the name of freedom but the Communist government they had replaced French colonialism with had made things even worse for the common man like himself.

Hoang's father had long ago given up fighting. Instead he raised his family by farming the land. This was all he had wanted from life and it made him happy.

Hoang could not find his father's weapon so he quickly dragged his father's body from the burning hootch to his mother. He looked into her tearful eyes without saying a word and left to follow the Americans, and to avenge his father's death.

Hoang's thoughts came back to the present while still staring at the gun. He knew what must be done. He cocked the gun and placed the muzzle near his left bicep. He closed his eyes, and squeezed off a round. His comrades could not believe what they'd just seen and ran over to him.

There was a lot of bleeding at first but it slowed to a trickle in a few seconds. The wound was not serious, he had merely grazed a large chunk of muscle. His friends bandaged the wound with a piece of cloth and finally asked him what had happened.

Hoang told them that he was willing to take extreme risks in order to get Tray back. He was going to walk right onto the

Americans' base pretending to be a wounded Montagnard in need of medical assistance.

The three young men set out for the Rock Pile Firebase with a look of grim determination on their faces. They knew their chances of success were not good. They walked along the sides of the mountain ridges keeping themselves hidden as much as possible from both the sky and the road which led to the base. When they got within sight of the base they looked for an area that was both high up and had good cover to use as a base camp.

Hoang told his friends to stay there and keep out of sight until he returned. He gave them his small Chinese made collapsible telescope and told them that if they saw the Americans kill him they were to leave immediately, and tell his family of his death. If not they were to remain in their position for two days and two nights. If he was not back by then they were to assume he was dead. Hoang told them under no circumstances were they to come after him because he did not want to be responsible for their deaths. They had more than enough rice and water to wait out the time.

Hoang gave them all the equipment he had which might give him away as being VC, said good-bye to his friends and slowly walked off toward the American fire base carrying nothing but an M16, his trusty 45, and lots of ammunition.

As he neared the base he started walking on the road. This felt very strange to him. It had been years since he'd walked an open road in broad daylight. He heard a truck convoy rumbling up behind him. His first instinct was to run for cover. He forced himself to relax though and kept on walking at a casual pace as though he belonged where he was.

As the driver of the first truck pulled up next to Hoang he noticed the fresh blood which had soaked through the cloth bandage on Hoang's arm. The driver instantly recognized Hoang as a friendly Montagnard and stopped to give him a lift.

Hoang was scared at first. He was walking down the side of the road eyes straight ahead, afraid to look at the Americans. When he noticed the truck stop alongside him he froze for a second before he turned to look into the cab of the huge American truck. He figured he was safe when he realized the soldier wasn't pointing a gun at him. Hoang saw a big, muscular American with a smile on his face. He was gesturing with his arm and yelling at Hoang to hop in.

Hoang seized the opportunity. In a flash his problem had been solved. This was his ticket into the American base. Hoang climbed up into the cab and said "Numba one GI" they saluted each other and the truck convoy started back up the winding dirt road, now only a short distance from the Rock Pile Firebase.

They pulled into the base, through the concentric lines of wire and bunkers, past the guards stationed at the main gate, and into the compound to the spot where the supplies of artillery rounds, ammunition and food were to be unloaded.

Hoang couldn't believe how lucky he'd been getting into the base, weapons and all. He sat in the cab of the truck trying to figure out what to do next. The driver gave him a friendly slap on his good arm and said "come on, I'll show ya to the aid station where they can fix up that arm."

"Bac she?" Said Hoang.

"Ya, that's right, bac she. Come on let's go."

Hoang followed the driver to the aid station but when they got there no one was in. "What kind of a place is this?" Said the driver, "come on let's go to HQ and find out where the Doc is."

"Bac she HQ?" Said Hoang.

"He better be" said the big blond truck driver from California. "Come on let's go."

The truck driver pounded his big fist several times on the Head Quarters door, after a short wait Fingers came to the door, before he'd really looked out he yelled "What the fuck do you want?", and then seeing the size of the Californian standing before him he said

"Howdy." in a little more friendly voice. Then noticing Hoang he said "Say is that a Yard you've got with ya?

"Genuine.", said California, "Straight out of the mountains and with a wound here good enough for a purple heart."

"Hey we could use this guy." said Fingers, "Come on in."

"By the way," said the truck driver, "where's y'ur goddammedic?"

"Don't blame it on me big guy," said Fingers, "I'm not even stationed here, but I hear he's on R and R. Hey, it's a bitch, I couldn't even get aspirin for my hangover this mornin'."

Hearing all the commotion The Monkey Man wandered in to see what was up. "All right, Fingers my man, ya found us a Yard. Man do we need him." The Monkey Man walked up to Hoang and shook his hand, "Welcome aboard."

The truck driver broke in, "Say we were just over to the aid station and the place was empty. This man needs a little medical attention."

"No problem" said The Monkey Man, "A couple of medics just drove in less than an hour ago. They're sacked out in the next room right now,"

The Monkey Man went to wake up Doc and Cyrano. It was not an easy task. He finally showed up ten minutes later with Doc and his medical bag. Cyrano just plain refused to move.

Doc looked terrible, his eyes were glowing red and he was having a tough time just trying to keep his balance. He looked at Hoang's wound and then looked back to The Monkey Man. "I need water" he said. Within a few seconds The Monkey Man was back with a full canteen of water. Doc grabbed it from him, put it to his mouth, tilted his head back and guzzled down the whole thing without stopping. When he finished, and leveled his head back down again, he had to throw both arms out just to keep his balance and not fall over.

Doc handed the canteen back to the Monkey Man and said "Thank you."

The Monkey Man just stared at him in disbelief. Finally he asked "You all right?"

Doc growled, "Just fine now." and went to work on Hoang's arm.

As Doc was cleaning the shallow wound with disinfectant he noticed powder burns on Hoang's arm and said to him "It looks like you must have been in some real shit, hand to hand combat no less."

Hoang seemed to understand and shouted back "me kill boo coo VC."

The Monkey Man patted Hoang on the back and said "All right man you're my kind of soldier. Where's the rest of your unit?" Hoang looked a little confused at first while he thought of what to say. The Monkey Man just thought he was having trouble understanding English. Finally he said, "All dead, I fight alone now."

"I'm sorry," said The Monkey Man, "but I'll tell you what, we could sure use a man like you. We can pay you in American dollars. We've got boo coo food and the best weapons money can buy. What da ya say man?"

Hoang looked a little confused again. He looked out the window to the mountain ranges off to the great northwest. The Americans weren't at all like he'd expected them to be. To his great surprise he liked them. They were very friendly, and seemed like good and honorable men. He actually wanted to join them, and he could use the money. Then a brilliant idea came to him. He turned to The Monkey Man, looked him in the eye and said "Need woman."

The Monkey Man looked at him and said "We've got one for ya right here, no problem."

Doc gave The Monkey Man a slightly surprised look and then finished putting a field dressing on Hoang's arm. The Monkey Man looked at Doc and said, "Good job. We'll have to make some kind of a deal with you guys for one of the whores you brought up here."

Doc was so out of it he didn't really care. "That's fine with me but I guess you'll have to talk with Cyrano about it."

"No problem" said The Monkey Man. "Cyrano will make a deal with us all right, I know the man."

"I've got to get some sleep" said Doc, "and this time I'd appreciate it if you not bother me for at least a couple of hours."

"Sorry Doc" said The Monkey Man, "but the medic from the base here is on R and R and they haven't sent a replacement for him yet."

Doc turned and walked away without saying a word. He was beginning to wonder if this so called mission was really such a good idea when he really could be on R and R, and someplace a little more sane than this, someplace like Bangkok maybe. Doc didn't think about this for too long though. He was too tired to think and fell back to sleep in a matter of seconds.

The Monkey Man took Hoang to the back rooms where the girls were working and told him he could pick out any one of the three for himself. He brought the three girls into a back hallway away from the lines of men outside.

Tray was so shocked when she saw Hoang that she actually gasped out loud. At first she thought he must have been taken prisoner until she noticed how friendly the big American Special Forces sergeant was acting towards him. Then she didn't know what to think.

"Well Hoang take your pick" said The Monkey Man. Hoang pretended to ignore Tray. He looked over the other two girls thoroughly and then looked as though he was about to choose one of them. Tray was almost starting to cry when Hoang seemed to suddenly change his mind and choose Tray. Tray threw her arms around Hoang as the tears welled up in her eyes. She didn't know exactly what was happening but she was very happy to see Hoang again.

"Jeese" said The Monkey, "you two look as though you've met before."

"Long time ago," said Hoang.

"Well that's great" said The Monkey Man. "She's all yours now and you can have the rest of the day off to heal your wound." The Monkey Man then showed them to a private room, pointed out the mess hall and told him to be ready for a mission at sunrise the next morning. The Monkey Man left them alone with a wink and a smile, then headed back to check up on the lines of men where Fingers was collecting the money. Ten dollars a head was a high price to pay and the soldiers were grumbling. The Monkey Man knew he could get away with it though because of the remote location of the Rock Pile Firebase. This far from civilization there was no competition.

When Tray and Hoang were finally alone she asked him in a disbelieving voice "What are you doing here?"

Hoang answered "I almost killed you by accident on the road. Luckily I saw you at the last instant before I pulled the trigger. When I figured out what they were using you for I made up my mind that I would sneak onto the American base and help you escape even if I had to die trying. I tried to look like a Montagnard and it worked so well they hired me to work with them. They said they will pay me in American dollars but I told them I must also have you and they agreed to it."

"Hoang, you know I had no choice but to work like this after I was captured?"

"Yes, I know" said Hoang as he put his arms around her.

"What happened to your arm?" She asked.

"Oh it was nothing."

CHAPTER 5
THE BELL TOLLS

"Say Fingers," said The Monkey Man "you know we'll have to have that chopper ready to go by nightfall."

"Yea, I know" said Fingers. "That flat black paint we ordered came in with the supply convoy."

"Special Forces black!" Said The Monkey Man.

"Roger that. Why don't you take over collecting the money and I'll go get it done." Fingers handed the money over to The Monkey Man. He kept one hundred dollars for himself and walked out into the crowd of GIs milling around in front of the whore shack. He held up the cash waving it in the air. "I need ten men to help me do a little job" he yelled out. "I'll pay any man five dollars an hour for a few hours work, anyone interested follow me." Fingers walked off towards the stolen helicopter not even bothering to look back.

A number closer to twenty men started to follow him. After a short distance the men turned and sort of checked each other out. There was an argument, and a few of the men turned and walked back to the whore shack. Then there was a longer and much louder argument followed by a confused fist fight. There were several bloodied noses and even a few men left unconscious in the red dirt. Ten men then left and double timed it to catch up with Fingers who was now waiting for them under the camouflage netting.

Back at the sight of the fist fight one of the men whose nose had been bloodied surveyed the unconscious men strewn about him. After a few seconds though he came to an inevitable conclusion. He yelled out as loud as he could "*Medic*!" Doc stirred in a restless sleep.

At the chopper Fingers had ten men already working at full tilt painting an olive drab Huey helicopter flat black, or special forces black as Fingers called it. At the same time he had a few other men loading supplies of ammunition and weapons into the chopper. He took the liberty of unloading Cyrano's jeep while he was at it,

Charlie Rats, slang for C-Rations, canned food for use in the field, and all.

It was an amazing sight to behold. The speed at which the men were working was incredible. The whole operation looked like a giant ant farm. They finished the job in two hours.

Back at the HQ a young private was trying to shake Doc back into consciousness. He kept saying "You're a doc ain't you? Wake up!"

Doc thought the base had been overrun and he was being beat to death by some crazed gook. He kept trying to open his eyes but they just wouldn't work. Finally both his ears and eyes began working at the same time. He looked at the young private and blurted out "Yea, I'm a doc." He would have said anything to get the man to stop shaking him.

A few rooms away in the HQ office Colonel Travis was on the radio talking to the Tactical Operations Command (TOC) bunker in Dong Ha. They were speaking in phonetic code to fool the enemy even though they both knew they weren't fooling anybody. Colonel Travis had been rudely awakened from his hangover at twelve hundred hours by his Radio Telephone Operator (RTO). He was a bit groggy as he listened to the bad news coming in from Dong Ha.

The gist of the message was that reconnaissance planes had spotted boo coo enemy troop movement in his AO. A division to brigade sized unit of North Vietnamese regular army troops had been spotted heading towards the Rock Pile Firebase.

Colonel Travis already had his big guns, the one five five howitzers, firing on the reported coordinates of the position. He was waiting for the spotter plane to fly back over the area and confirm the success of his fire mission. TOC finally came back on the line with his answer. The plane reported that his guns had been well aimed, a bulls eye right on the money. Only problem was the enemy had somehow disappeared. There was no body count and no sign of any enemy activity anywhere in the surrounding area.

Colonel Travis's eyes glazed over, he was visibly shaken by the report. He went back on the radio and asked TOC for help. He needed reinforcements for his fire base. He was severely under manned and knew that he did not stand a chance against a force that large. He asked TOC if they could send in some Marines.

"No can do" the answer came back. "The Marines have left the area for good. They're down south in Da Nang and their plans are to leave country as soon as possible."

"What about the Rangers?" Asked Colonel Travis.

"Sorry they're on a mission in the Northwest Territory."

"Dammit" said Travis. "There aren't any Cav units close enough and they can't go up those mountain roads at night. The earliest they could get here would be late morning and by then we'd all be dead."

"There is one thing we can do for ya" said TOC. "We have a B-52 strike scheduled for the DMZ late this afternoon. We can divert them to your AO. They'll make a moonscape out of everything between the Rock Pile and the NVA's last reported position."

"Roger that" said Colonel Travis "it's our only hope but I don't think it will work. Those Dinks really know how to dig in and they've got caves all over this area."

"We'll do everything we can for ya Colonel Travis. The B-52's are on their way and so is the Cav. Before night fall we'll have Fire Base Alpha's big guns trained on your perimeter. That's all we can do Colonel Travis, I just hope it's enough. It's a damn tough war Travis, gook luck! Dong Ha TOC out."

At five o'clock the bell tolled from the mess hall. The black chopper was loaded and ready to go. The lines from the whore shack were just about down to nil and most of the men started moving towards the smell of hot chow when suddenly the ground began to shake. At first some of the men thought it must be an earthquake until they recognized the distinctively loud sound of five hundred pound bombs exploding.

The men looked at each other with questioning looks in their eyes until the realization began to sink in. Some of them looked up and were just barely able to make out the shining silver shapes of B-52 bombers. They were used to watching the B-52's work out, but none of them had ever seen the bombs land this close.

There was fear in the young soldiers eyes as they ran to their hootches and dug through their personal gear looking for what was important. Helmets, flack jackets and weapons. A line was quickly forming at the ammunition shack and without any orders being given many of the men were taking up positions at the bunkers and trenches along the perimeter of the small fire base.

The line at the chow hall was forming much later than usual and was only half the normal length. The men standing in it were loaded down with M-16's and bandoleers of ammunition.

The usual laughing and joking had been replaced by an uneasy silence with occasional subdued whispers.

Back at the HQ hootch Fingers and The Monkey Man were with Colonel Travis who was at the radio waiting for another situation report. "This must be the major offensive the Company boys (CIA) were talking about at the Ranch" said The Monkey Man.

"No doubt about it" said Fingers, "even the Company's worried about this one. They say there's thirty thousand Chinese troops stationed in the Northwest Territory and they're afraid they might try to surround the Ranch."

"Christ", said Colonel Travis. "This sounds like it could be the start of World War Three."

"I think it's already started" said The Monkey Man.

Just then the radio broke squelch and Dong Ha TOC came on with a negative situation report. "No body count from the B-52 strike and no sign of the enemy. We know they're out there someplace though. We've had boo coo intelligence reports on this one. They're launching a major offensive in Northern I Corps."

"We are truly fucked" said Colonel Travis.

"Watch your radio language" said TOC. "A large Troop sized unit of the Cav is on their way to your position and They're going to attempt to climb that mountain road tonight."

"They'll never make it" Colonel Travis came back.

"They volunteered for the mission and they're highly motivated. They'll make it. We just hope they can make it in time. You've got to hold on until they get there Colonel Travis, we're doing everything we can for ya. TOC out."

Colonel Travis looked at The Monkey Man and said "Maybe you guys should leave while you still have a chance."

"I don't mind flying at night it's probably safer than in day light as long as we keep our lights out. The only problem is trying to land up there in the dark. They've got boo coo NVA in their AO too. At night they have a tendency to come in close to the Ranch. They'll have RPGs in the wire for sure and we'll make the perfect target. No Colonel we'll hang on here as long as we can, besides we can't leave an old friend like you when you're in trouble"

"Bull shit" said Colonel Travis.

Doc and Cyrano had overheard the entire conversation from the next room where they had spent most of the day attempting to sleep. "It looks like we're totally fucked no matter what we do" said Cyrano.

"I knew I should have gone to Australia or Bangkok for my R and R" said Doc.

They had both had an instant wake up from deep sleep when the ground began shaking from the B-52 strike. It was a very disorienting wake up. "But just think Doc" said Cyrano, "you can go to Australia or Bangkok anytime. How many chances in your lifetime do you think you'll be able to visit the ancient kingdom of Siam?"

"I'm not so sure I even want to see this strange place you call Siam" said Doc. "It sounds a bit dangerous."

Just then Hoang and Tray walked in. "Siam is Thailand," Hoang said "Laos was called Lan Xang, Land of Million Elephants and Hmong people you fight for escaped from China only few generations ago. According to legends they landed on Magic Mountain that you call The Rock on flying carpet."

"Flying carpet?" Said Cyrano.

"There you go" said Doc. "You don't even know where we're going."

"Flying carpet!" Said Cyrano, "This is even better than I thought."

Hoang flexed the muscles in his wounded arm and said "Thank you Doc, arm much better now."

Doc just smiled and said "I think your girl friend there might have had something to do with that."

"Monkey Man say you came on mission too" said Hoang. "Yea, I guess so" said Doc looking at Cyrano.

"We must leave soon" said Hoang, "Boo coo NVA come here."

"Yea we know" said Doc.

CHAPTER 6
THE CAV AND THE ALAMO

Back at Dong Ha, B Troop of the Cav was saddling up. It was Doc's old Troop. KC climbed into the cupola of track three three and said to Fred sitting along side of him "I'm way too short for these night time expeditions. Fifteen days and a wake up!" KC had taken over as track commander of three three after Red's death from the fraging, which is to say that he was killed by his own men with a fragmentation grenade. KC often had intense feelings of anger over the incident, and trouble sleeping because of that anger. Deep inside he wanted revenge, he wanted to kill someone.

The men had been on stand down, coming in from the field for several days of rest. They hadn't really volunteered for this mission to The Rock Pile. Their Captain had done that for them. They weren't too happy about it but there wasn't much they could do to stop it. It was their job and they excepted it with mild grunts of complaint.

The Captain was getting short too. His six months in the field were just about up. One more well accomplished mission would look good on his record. A night time combat assault into enemy held territory and the rescue of a fire base from being overrun would win him his Colonel's leafs for sure. It was a risky operation but he figured he had to do it to further his career. He knew there would be some losses and that saddened him. He also knew the job could be done, and hoped he could keep his losses low.

The Captain looked out over his line of APCs (Armored Personnel Carriers) and Sheridan tanks. When he'd seen that they were all saddled up he gave the command to begin. "Foreword haooo!"

Several of the more gung ho men answered back with "yea haa," as the tracks quickly accelerated to their maximum speed. Time was of the essence now if the Cav was to save the lives of the men at the Rock Pile. They would have to keep up this speed until the mountains slowed them down. With a little luck they would reach the Rock Pile before dawn and hopefully before the base was overrun. In the nick of time!

At the fire base things were too quiet. It was the quiet before the storm and the men all new it. Cyrano walked to Colonel Travis' office and gently rapped on the open door. The three men looked at him. Cyrano started to speak a little nervously "Ahh, say Monkey Man, the Doc and me have finished our beauty sleep and we were wondering if we're gonna leave this place before all hell breaks loose."

"I'm afraid we can't 'till o-four hundred hours" said The Monkey Man. "That is assuming there's any of us still left alive."

"That bad?" Said Cyrano.

" 'Fraid so" said The Monkey Man.

"Say Cyrano" said Colonel Travis. "I think it would be a good idea if you and the other Doc would set up shop in the aid station for tonight. The place is well supplied with medical equipment and we'll probably need it all before the night's over. You'll be free to leave at o-four hundred hours. By then I don't think it'll matter much anymore. And by the way, grab yourselves some hot chow at the mess hall while you still have a chance. Your gonna need all the energy you can get before the night's over."

"Roger that" said Cyrano. "We'll do what we can."

"This doesn't look good at all" said Doc a few moments later as he and Cyrano spoke back at the bunks. He told Doc about his short conversation with the powers that be, his head bowed with concern. Doc stood up and said "Well, let's do it." Cyrano turned his gaze from the floor to Tray and Hoang. "Why don't you two come with us. It looks like we're gonna need all the help we can get."

Tray began to realize the seriousness of their situation. "We get my friends, they can help."

The four of them headed off to the whore shack, picked up the other two, and the six of them walked together to the aid station where Doc and Cyrano found and organized the medical equipment. It appeared as though the place was well stocked with everything they would need. "It looks like they've been through this before", Doc said to Cyrano.

Doc showed the women how to use the pressure bandages and tourniquets to stop bleeding. Then he showed them some basic CPR. Doc himself would be in charge of IV's and administration of morphine. Cyrano would handle Triage, deciding who should be worked on first and who was too badly wounded to bother with. They would be made as comfortable as possible but unfortunately left to die. Hoang would guard the entrance to the heavily sand bagged aid station to stop any NVA Sappers, enemy commando armed with explosive satchel charges, who might get through the perimeter of the fire base. From the looks of things this would be a highly probable situation.

When everyone looked as though they understood the game plan they all headed off to see what was left to eat. Like Colonel Travis said they would need all the energy they could get.

The usual line was gone by the time they arrived at the mess hall and although there were still several men sitting at the tables eating the place had a deserted feel to it. They walked through the screen door and when it slammed behind them suddenly all eyes turned to them. The men looked suspicious of the six odd looking strangers among them. Doc thought he caught a glimpse of racial prejudice in some of their looks, or maybe it was just his imagination. He still wasn't felling right after those weird green beret pills and on top of that he hadn't had enough sleep. Doc guessed they didn't really fit in, in this place. In war men can become superstitious and weary of even the smallest change in their environment because of the extreme stress of their predicament.

Doc figured the men's feelings toward them would change soon enough when they started saving their lives. This was going to be one hell of a night!

It started early, real early for what Doc had been used to with the Cav. As a matter of fact the NVA didn't even give the sky a chance to go completely black after sunset. They started with mortars, a few unfortunate men were hit by shrapnel right off the bat. Cyrano managed to recruit ten men as stretcher bearers and by the time the rockets and RPGs started to come in an hour later those ten men had an almost constant line of wounded coming in, including two of the stretcher bearers themselves.

The aid station quickly turned into a scene of total chaos. The women were doing an unbelievable job, but the wounded were stacking up on the floor all around them. By twenty-two hundred Doc had given up on IV's and morphine. He'd run out of both. Men were dying from loss of blood before anyone could get to them and plug up the holes. They were all working as fast as they could but it wasn't fast enough.

Just then they heard a blast of M16 fire followed closely by a large explosion. These came from directly outside the aid station door and they were followed by a scream of "Sappers through the wire!" then more small arms fire from both AK47s and M16s.

The blast just outside the aid station had come from Hoang, he killed the first sapper's suicidal mission. The sapper had instinctively triggered his satchel charge as soon as he was hit hoping at least to kill anyone near him, but Hoang had quickly ducked behind the sand bags surrounding the aid station. Hoang popped back up from his cover and began firing again. The enemy swarmed everywhere. They had overrun the base and were fighting hootch to hootch. The men were hidden anywhere they could find cover, mainly behind sand bag walls.

The wounded finally stopped coming in which gave Doc and his crew a chance to catch up with them. They just had things under control when they heard small arms fire directly in front of the aid station. It was Fingers and The monkey man. They had fought their way across the compound. They ran through the aid station door guarded by Hoang and told the two medics it was time to leave. Doc didn't want to go, he didn't want to leave all those wounded men behind. Cyrano and Fingers each grabbed one of his arms and started dragging him out the door while The Monkey Man whispered in his ear "You can't help anybody if you're dead." Doc grabbed his M16 and the eight of them began to slowly fight their way across the base to the waiting chopper.

The air was thick with bullets, they whizzed by like swarms of bees. The group stopped at each sand bag wall they came to along the way and shot up anything that moved. When they thought all heads were down they continued on to the next wall. With a great deal of luck they all made it to the chopper without being hit.

The spot was well guarded. The chopper was hidden behind sandbag walls and the entire circle was manned by well armed soldiers who were holding their fire as much as possible to conserve ammunition.

Cyrano looked at his watch. It was o-two hundred hours. Half jokingly he looked at The Monkey Man and said "it's only two o'clock how come we're leaving so early."

In complete seriousness The Monkey Man answered back "The Cav's on their way and we've got to get out before they show up. Those guys are dangerous."

Doc broke into the conversation. "What ever happened to our artillery support from Firebase Alpha?"

The Monkey Man answered back "They were overrun at the same time we were. The NVA have got a major offensive going here."

"No shit." said Cyrano.

"Say Fingers," the Monkey Man said. "when we take off keep your eye on our guards. I've got a feeling they might try to jump on the chopper with us and we're already at maximum load capacity. You're gonna have to keep'em off the skids no matter what it takes."

"Roger that" said Fingers.

Then The Monkey Man yelled out "all right gang, is everybody ready?" They all nodded their heads. "Let's mount up." With that all eight of them jumped aboard the helicopter and The Monkey Man fired it up. The roar from the engine instantly drew enemy fire to the circle of sandbags. The Monkey Man revved the engine and started to lift off as fast as the chopper would allow. They were just off the ground when the guards all decided they wanted out of the hell hole they were in and made a mad rush for the open door of the chopper.

Fingers was waiting for them with his AK-47. He swung the thing like a baseball bat hitting the first man in the head and knocking him to the ground. The other men slowed down until the chopper was almost out of reach. At the last second several of them jumped up and grabbed the skids of the chopper stopping its upward motion. Just then several enemy AK rounds slammed through the skin of the chopper with a metallic clank and the sound of breaking glass. Fingers bent over the side wildly flailing his wooden stocked AK at the guards. He started sliding out the door, Doc and Cyrano grabbed his legs just as an RPG whooshed through the open doors of the chopper and out the other side without touching a thing, but leaving smoke and the smell of burned cordite (modern gun powder) inside the cabin.

The Monkey Man yelled back from the pilots seat "you're gonna have to waste 'em Fingers!"

The Monkey Man had a commanding loud voice, and over the years they'd known each other, Fingers had become in tune with it so that even above the inhumanly loud noises of the chopper and the combat going on around them Fingers heard exactly what The Monkey Man had said. Just the thought of it brought tears to his eyes. To kill his own men, fellow Americans, this he could not do. The thought of it brought a feeling of rage to his entire being giving him the strength of ten men. He yelled out a scream that could be heard above the roar of the battle field "Noooo!" He flailed away ferociously at the men and they dropped to the ground freeing the helicopter which quickly flew away escaping the insanity of war at least for a short time. Fingers lay on the floor of the chopper with tears streaming down his mud caked face. The Monkey Man had played him for everything he was worth, and they had all survived!

CHAPTER 7
CAVALRY TO THE RESCUE

The Monkey Man was worried. The Cav should have arrived at the Rock Pile by now. He knew something was wrong. They must have been ambushed somewhere along the narrow mountain road. He decided to follow the road and see what had happened to them.

Fingers got on the radio and tuned in the Cav's frequency. The channel was filled with the sounds of chaos. The lead Sheridan had been hit by an RPG and was blocking the road. They were pinned down under heavy AK47 fire. The Captain had been radioing for artillery and gunship support but none was available. Fingers got on the net. "This is White Star from the Rock Pile we're on our way to your position with one gunship, we'll be there in two mikes (military phonetic code for two minutes)."

The Monkey Man followed the winding mountain road as best he could in the dark. They hadn't gone far before they started to see the Cav's red tracer rounds slicing through the night sky. Fingers and Cyrano got on the two sixty caliber machine guns. One of the Cav track commanders fired a white phosphorous round from an M79 grenade launcher to mark the suspected NVA position in the rocks up above them. The tracks and tanks had trouble aiming their guns that high up from their fixed positions.

Fingers and Cyrano both opened up on the burning white phosphorous. The Monkey Man had installed some rockets on the chopper back at the Rock Pile, he armed them and dove in on the position firing two rockets accurately at the spot. The enemy fire stopped and the track behind the disabled Sheridan tank pushed it off the side of the mountain. The Cav troop moved out at top speed toward the fire base with the chopper flying above them.

Hoang had been quietly sitting on the floor of the chopper with Tray and the two whores. He was beginning to have his doubts about joining in with these strange Americans. They were friendly enough to him all right but they were waging war on his people or at least half of his people. Which side was right? He had heard their political arguments and both sides' propaganda had made sense to him but he was beginning to think they must both be very wrong. No form of government could possibly be worth all this killing, it was insanity. Then there was Tray.

Hoang's thoughts turned to his two VC cell member friends. Although the Cav ambush was not in their area it could have just as easily been them. He looked down at the winding mountain road beneath the chopper and suddenly realized the Cav was just about to his friend's position.

Doc looked down at his clothes, they were covered with blood. For a second he wondered if any of it was his but he didn't have the energy to check himself for holes. The last thing he wanted was another one of those green beret pills. The realization struck him that those damn pills were probably the reason he was here. Without them he most likely would have passed out sometime after midnight and would have slept right through this shit.

Hoang slapped Doc on the back and gave him a thumbs up sign with a smile. Doc wearily smiled back and was struck by a second realization. It was obvious that Hoang and Tray had known each other for quite some time. Which meant that he was probably VC and most likely he was the same VC who had escaped from the Cav at both Mai Loc and the Rock Pile just a few weeks ago. Docs smile faded.

Hoang stood up and tapped Cyrano on the shoulder gesturing toward the sixty caliber machine gun. Cyrano said "be my guest, I was never very good at this sort of thing." Hoang took over the sixty just as an explosion and fireball erupted off the back of the lead track below them. Fortunately it did not penetrate the light armor of the track. It just glanced off and exploded. Hoang quickly opened up with the sixty carefully placing the red tracer rounds away from the position of his two friends. The Cav didn't even slow down, they opened up on the spot Hoang was firing at as they sped by.

Hoang's two VC friends lay on the rocky ground behind a bolder and marveled at their luck. The Cav's awesome firepower wasn't even coming close to them. Even so the sight of all those tracer rounds slamming into the rocks along side them was enough to keep them from firing their RPG again.

As the Cav finally approached the Rock Pile Firebase from a distance it looked like a seen from hell. The rubber blevit fuel tank was ablaze and it lit the night sky with its dancing red flames. Satchel charges and American grenades were exploding everywhere. Green tracers from NVA AK47s and red ones from M16s were intermixed from every possible position. Men's screams could be heard above the sound of the tracks as they roared into the melee.

At the Perimeter wire the tracks positioned themselves on line and started a slow sweep through the compound. As they moved through the green tracers seemed to organize at the opposite side of the fire base and then slowly fade away to nothing as they disappeared into the heavy vegetation beyond the far side of the base.

The Monkey Man radioed to Captain Black of the Cav. "Go get 'em boys, I've got business to attend to."

Captain Black radioed back, "Thanks for the help White Star, whoever you are!" With that the chopper banked to the west its nose tilted down and it accelerated to the west as the first rays of the morning sun began to paint the sky pink behind them.

CHAPTER 8
SHANGRI-LA

The earth below them turned more mountainous and rugged as they flew. Somehow the land became more primitive as though they were flying backwards in time. They flew on. Doc looked down at a mountain top and saw a flock of giant birds circling around it. The birds looked almost reptilian, like Pterodactyls from prehistoric times. He shook his head thinking he must be dreaming but when he looked back they were still there. Cyrano turned to Doc and yelled "it looks like dinosaur country down there. I wouldn't be surprised to see old Tyrannosaurus Rex himself poke his head up from behind one of those mountain peaks."

The mountains slowly started to level off when the passengers noticed in the distance a sheer rock cliff rising up from the valley floor almost like a man-made sky scraper, only much too large. It was on a whole other scale. On a scale of giants, or maybe gods.

Hoang and the girls looked in awe. They bowed to it in unison and whispered Phou Pha Thi. It looked as if they were paying their respects to a god. Doc thought maybe if not a god it must surely be a monument to a god.

Fingers yelled out "Watch your asses people. We're comin' up on the Rock, the most valuable piece of real estate in all of southeast Asia, and I'm sorry to say it's owned by the bad guys who are well armed."

The Monkey Man steered the chopper in a wide arc around the place. He yelled out to the back of the chopper "the Hmong people who we've been working with here believe that this is a sacred mountain. Our Air Force put a radar installation there a few years ago to guide out B-52s into Hanoi. The NVA scaled those cliffs and over ran the place. They have owned it ever since. The Hmong have been trying to take it back. They don't think we can win this war until we do and I think they're right. I hate to be the one to break this to you boys but I'm afraid we're losing this war and unless we can get some ground troops into this area soon we never will win it."

The chopper continued on to the west. No one said a word for quite some time. Finally Doc broke the silence. "It's all politics. The REMFs (Rear Echelon Mother Fuckers) back in Washington are just afraid they won't get re-elected if they don't pull us out of here. They know damn well the South Vietnamese don't stand a chance without us."

"I can't believe they're gonna just let us lose a war" said Cyrano.

"There it is" said The Monkey Man nodding towards the Rock. They continued on again in silence for quite some time. Finally the mountainous terrain gave way to a large expanse of flat ground, a high plateau. It was the most beautiful sight Doc had ever seen, covered with bright red flowers (opium poppies). Butterflies and wild game seemed to be everywhere, it was an awe inspiring sight. "This must be it", said Cyrano. "The Plain of Jars."

"Shangri-la!" Said The Monkey Man. "If it exists anywhere on this planet this has got to be the place." The Monkey Man took the chopper down low to the ground. "I still don't see those mysterious jars", he said.

"They've got to be hear someplace", said Cyrano.

"I know where jars are" said Hoang. "They're southwest near the CIA base at Long Tieng."

"CIA base?" Said Doc.

"That's supposed to be top secret information" said The Monkey Man. "The only people who seem to know about it are the NVA." The Monkey Man made eye contact with Hoang. Hoang quickly looked away and thought to himself that maybe he wasn't fooling anyone after all.

"We don't have enough fuel to search for them now, and besides we've got a business appointment at the Ranch to take care of." With that The Monkey Man swung the chopper to the north towards the mountains which surrounded the plain. Doc thought to himself that Shangri-la seemed to be a strange place for a secret CIA base.

The black ship came up to the mountains low and had to climb to keep from running into them. The Monkey Man had to give the chopper all the power it had in the thin atmosphere with such a heavy load, "I still don't think you've learned how to fly this thing." said Fingers. "It's lucky we got rid of those rockets back at the Rock Pile or I don't think we'd be able to make this climb."

"Damn lucky just to be alive from the Rock Pile is more like it", said Doc.

"Seemed more like a miracle to me", said Cyrano.

"Awe tawern't nothin'.", said Fingers.

"Bullshit.", said Cyrano.

There was no sign of any kind of base as the chopper labored to gain altitude. No trails were even visible along the face of the mountain in front of them. Finally they broke over the top of the mountain and followed the flat rocky ridge straight ahead about two feet off the ground. There was a base all right and no one there had noticed the black helicopter 'till it was on them. There hadn't been time for them to.

The Monkey Man had to gain a few more feet in height to keep from hitting one of the perimeter guards who at the time was looking in the opposite direction. As they flew directly over his head the poor man nearly had a heart attack. He screamed and hit the dirt, face down. There was a small group of men waiting in a chow line. They heard the scream but by the time they turned around to look the chopper was already on them, they hit the ground in surprise also. As the chopper banked away towards the landing zone one of the troops on the ground yelled out "Looks like Fingers and The Monkey Man got us another chopper!"

The Monkey Man hovered the chopper at a dead still over the LZ (landing zone) for a few seconds and then slowly lowered her down until the skids gently touched the ground. As the motley crew of men and women disembarked from the helicopter they were met by a Green Beret Captain, several NCOs, and a number of men dressed in civilian clothing. "Looks like your troops here have been through hell" said the captain, "and I'm afraid you've purchased some damaged goods. This chopper is all full of holes."

"Don't mean nothin' ", said The Monkey Man, "it still flies good."

"Oh yea?" Said a voice from a crowd of men standing behind the NCOs "it just about killed me on its way in." At that the crowd broke into laughter.

"We'd better get this crew of yours cleaned up" the Captain said nodding at the blood soaked clothes that they were all wearing from the ordeal at the Rock Pile aid station. "Looks like you two managed to keep high and dry once again" said the captain referring to the fact that Fingers and The Monkey Man were the only ones among them with clean uniforms.

"My troops need breakfast and at least five hours of undisturbed rest" said The Monkey Man to the Special Forces Captain.

"It looks as if they've earned it" said the Captain, "but the first thing they need is some clean clothes and a shower. Take care of these men sergeant" said the Special Forces Captain to his supply sergeant and then he added "and the ladies too. They got a big job to do this evening so make sure they get everything they need."

"Yes sir!" Said the supply sergeant with a snappy salute which was returned in the same manor by the captain.

"And you two come with me" said the captain to Fingers and The Monkey Man. "We've got to make plans for that mission tonight. There have been some new developments that you guys might find interesting. There's something big going on down on the plain tonight and I just know you guys will want to be in on it."

As Doc and the rest of the crew followed the supply sergeant Doc looked around the base. There really wasn't much to it. most of the soldiers were made up of the local mountain people. Doc thought at first that they were Montagnards but when he called them that Hoang quickly corrected him with a slightly insulted look on his face. He called them Meo. He even seemed a little angered that Doc could not tell the difference.

One strange thing for a military base was the large number of women and children around going about their daily chores. This place was really more of a village than it was a military base. The few Americans Doc saw were an odd combination. Some of them were obviously Special Forces wearing their tiger stripe fatigues and green berets. There were others wondering around who looked almost like tourists wearing shorts and Hawaiian print sport shirts.

They walked by a small air strip which barely looked as though it had room for an airplane to land on. It was there they saw the strangest sight of all, old fashioned prop driven fighter planes. "Jeese" said Cyrano "maybe we really have gone back in time, those planes look like they're right out of World War Two."

"Yea, weird" said Doc. "Shangri-la?"

CHAPTER 9
OF RAVENS AND BAD AMMO

At the Ranch Headquarters hootch a meeting was going on. Fingers and The Monkey Man were being filled in on the latest enemy troop movements down on the plain. The men who looked like tourists were there. They worked for Air America, the CIA owned airline. There were also a few Air Force pilots dressed in their flight suits which bore no identifying insignia.

One of the Air Force pilots was pointing out an area on the map, "The Ravens first noticed the heavy troop concentration almost a week ago." The Ravens are Air Force FAC (observation) pilots stationed in Vietnam who volunteered to work with the CIA fighting a secret war in Laos. They wore no insignia and if shot down were disowned by the US "They actually had a bonfire burning right there in the middle of all those big old jars." He continued, "Well right away I figured they must be friendlies acting like that. Stupid friendlies maybe, giving their position away like that, but they sure as hell couldn't be NVA. I buzzed them a couple of times to see what was going on and they just ignored me, like I wasn't even there. It looked like they were holding some sort of a ceremony, maybe religious being around those old jars like that.

"I called into Long Tieng to find out if there were any friendlies in the area." He said. Long Tieng was a CIA headquarters in Laos that was not on any maps though it was the second largest city in Laos. It was commonly called the secret city. "They gave me a definite negative to that and said they must be either NVA or Chinese, most likely Chinese with a big fire like that burning. They're the only ones that would have the guts to do something like that. The NVA wouldn't be that stupid."

Fingers and The Monkey Man were listening to this account with great interest, wondering what would cause a large group of people to allow themselves to be so exposed right in the middle of a war.

"The area is considered a protected site because of the Jars," The pilot went on, "so Long Tieng had to get permission all the way from Washington in order to send out a bombing mission. The enemy activity continued in the same area for the next two days but only at night. By sunrise they disappear without a trace. On the third night we finally got permission straight from the White House for a bombing raid. B-52s were ruled out right away because of the excessive damage they would cause to the Jars. So a sortie of Sky raiders was finally sent out."

"I was working the area that night so when the Sky raiders showed up I dove in to drop a Willy Pete marker (white phosphorus used to mark a spot for the bombers to aim their bombs) on the spot for them. The marker round didn't go off so I tried several more runs and none of them lit up. Although we've never had the problem before I figured we must have had a bunch of defective rounds. All this time I hadn't received one round of enemy fire which sort of had me worried about whether they were really enemy troops."

"None the less though we had our orders straight from Washington so I had the Sky raiders follow me in to the spot and with the bonfire burning I guess we didn't really need the marker rounds anyway. Well they dropped some of their ordinance and nothing happened, not one explosion, not even a spark."

"We couldn't believe it. I went up high and watched them make several more runs on the target. They dropped everything they had without one round exploding and still no enemy fire."

"The Sky raiders called up to me, 'This is too weird to believe, get us the hell out of here Raven, our compasses are spinning like tops. Just point us in the right direction.' When we got back to Long Tieng we had the mechanics and ordinance personnel check everything out. They couldn't find anything wrong with the planes or any of the ordinance at the base."

"After finding no trace of them the next day we sent out another sortie again that night. This time things were even worse. As soon as we got close to the area we lost all radio contact. The compasses were spinning again and then our engines started cutting out. We turned back with our engines sputtering and just enough power to get out of there. We tried a couple more times with the same results and finally had to give up."

"Back in Washington they figured the Russians must have invented some sort of new weapon. That's when the decision was made to send the Rangers in to see if they could find out what was going on. The Rangers were dropped off at an LZ some distance away from the jars just before sunset. They headed into the area on foot and were ordered to give a radioed situation report on the hour. The first report came in as scheduled with no enemy movement in sight. That was the last thing we heard from them. We were hoping to re-establish radio contact this morning but it never happened. We sent a reconnaissance plane in just about an hour ago and he reported the area was completely deserted."

"We're assuming the Rangers are still there and hiding as they were ordered but with dead radios. Washington has made a decision to attack and capture as many of the enemy as possible tonight. They want to know what's going on here ASAP! What we've decided to do is to send someone in there before dark to give the Rangers the order."

After listening quietly The Monkey Man finally spoke up. "We can be ready to leave by 1500 hours."

"Rise and shine troops, we're movin' out! I said rise and shine!" Doc thought he was dreaming. He thought he was back in basic training and his drill sergeant was pacing the wooden floors up and down the barracks. Doc slowly opened his eyes, he felt terrible, every muscle in his body ached and he knew he needed one hell of a lot more sleep than he'd had.

"This has got to be basic training." He mumbled unintelligibly. Fingers was standing before him with his hands on his hips. He looked to Doc like some sort of a Drill Sergeant from hell with his green beret pulled down rakishly to one side. A scar on the side of his face stood out in the afternoon sun as it filtered through dusty screens on the walls of the plywood hootch. Doc and Cyrano slowly struggled out of their cots both trying to remember exactly where they were.

"The Jars," Fingers said "we're goin' to see the jars and there's some really strange shit goin' on down there. Come on you guys get your gear and let's get movin'. I'll meet you at the chopper in ten mikes."

"We're on our way" said Cyrano, as Fingers strolled out the door. Then Cyrano turned to Doc and said "Alright. This is our big chance we're gonna be rich, I can't fuckin' believe it."

"I just hope I don't fall asleep when we get there" said Doc.

"Ah come on Doc you'll be OK as soon as we get movin',

come on."

Doc struggled to get his gear together as Cyrano ranted and raved about what he was going to do when he got back to the World (The US of A) as a rich man. In ten minutes they were at the chopper waiting for the rest of the crew. "Say Cyrano" said Doc "have you noticed how these guys always seem to be late for their appointments."

"Maybe your watch is off" said Cyrano.

"In just ten minutes?" Said Doc "besides it's a Timex, it takes a lickin'. By the way Cyrano what makes you so sure there's going to be anything of value in those old jars?"

"Ancient civilizations have always buried their dead with their most valuable possessions so they could take them with to their next life in heaven or wherever it is they believe they go to. Just look at the Egyptians or even the American Indians for that matter."

"Maybe so" said Doc "but what if the only thing they considered to be valuable was hieroglyphics on old parchment paper?"

"Well, maybe we could sell them to a museum or something?"

"Yea, maybe" said Doc. "Hey, here they come and it looks like they're really loaded for bear."

Fingers, The Monkey Man and Hoang were walking swiftly and silently towards the chopper loaded down with full rucksacks on their backs. It was surprising how easily they carried all that weight. It was obvious they had spent a lot of time carrying those rucks. Behind them were the four helicopter crew members dressed in jump suits and wearing large Fiberglas helmets with dark tinted visors over their faces. They looked like men from mars and walked like it too. Almost like they couldn't quite get used to the heavier gravity of earth. Two of them were having a great deal of difficulty carrying a pair of extra rucksacks.

As they approached the chopper The monkey Man yelled out "You guys fired up?"

"Not really" said Doc.

"Well I'm afraid it's too late to back out now. There's a bunch of Rangers waiting for us down by the Jars and if everything goes as planned tonight odds are they'll need all the medics they can get."

"Great" said Doc sarcastically.

"By the way" said Fingers, pointing to the two extra rucks. "You guys are gonna have to wear these things."

"Here we'll help you put them on" said The Monkey Man. As one was heaved onto Docs back he growled "Aw man, I feel like a pack mule."

"There it fuckin' is" said Fingers.

With a little help Doc and Cyrano managed to climb aboard the chopper in their weighted down condition. "You mean we're actually supposed to walk with these things on?" Said Doc as he tried to sit down, and instead landed on his back with his arms and legs sticking straight up in the air.

"You look like a dead cockroach" said Cyrano.

"Not worry." said Hoang, "You get used to them."

"I don't think Doc wants to get used to them" said Cyrano, "and I know I don't want to."

"Say Monkey Man," said the chopper pilot, "You know I really appreciate you guys gettin' this new bird for us after our last one was shot down. But was it really necessary to get the thing all shot up before you even got it back to us?"

"Damn gooks were havin' a major offensive down in northern I Corp. Besides, I figured you'd feel more at home with it this way."

"Damn thoughtful of ya" said the pilot.

As the chopper lifted off The Monkey Man went over the plans for the mission. He didn't like them at all but in a situation as strange as this one was he didn't have any better ideas. What he didn't like about the orders was the fact that they were to land right at the jars and then search the area for some sort of new radio jamming device. If there really was something there the Russians or whoever owned it wouldn't just leave it unguarded. They would be sitting ducks out there with no cover but the jars themselves. It was a suicide mission!

CHAPTER 10
ANCIENT TRIBES

As the chopper approached the jars from a distance The Monkey Man attempted to make radio contact with the Rangers. He got no answer. He knew his radio was working because he was still in contact with both the Ranch and Long Tieng. They made a few low passes of the jars and could see no sign of enemy activity or the Rangers.

"This is weird" said Fingers. "It doesn't look like anybody's been around here for months. I just hope we're surrounded by Rangers out there and not NVA waiting to ambush us."

"There's only one way to know for sure" said The Monkey Man. "Lets set down and find out." Quickly and gently the chopper pilot set the black bird down next to the ancient jars. Five green men jumped out in the middle of nowhere and the chopper quickly lifted up and away.

"Lucky so far" said Fingers.

"OK troops" said the Monkey Man, "I want you to spread out and search this area thoroughly, let me know if you find anything unusual."

"These jars look damn unusual!" Said Cyrano.

"No shit" said Fingers.

"Hoang, what's wrong" said Doc. For the first time since they'd met Hoang looked scared.

"I've heard of this place before" said Hoang. "The Gods own this land. It is a place of much magic. I have heard it said the magic of these Gods is stronger than the Americans greatest weapons. We should treat this place with great respect."

"I hear ya" said Doc. "I get the same feelin' just lookin' at those jars."

"I guess I better use this thing" said The Monkey Man. "The CIA case officer who gave it to me made a big deal about it, said it came from the shop, CIA HQ." He unstrapped what looked like a metal or mine detector from his rucksack and showed it to Fingers. "This thing is supposed to detect any type of metal plus any kind of electromagnetic radiation including nuclear radiation."

"Hey, just like James Bond" said Fingers.

The Monkey Man flipped a switch and began searching the ground in front of him with it. "'Nothin'" he said.

"How 'bout checkin' one of those jars with it?" Said Cyrano.

"Sure" said The Monkey Man, "but according to the Case Officer there's nothing to those things but stone and bone, they checked them out years ago, said they even tried to lift one out with one of the big choppers. They wanted to bring it back to the world and use it as a tomb for the unknown Case Officer but they couldn't even budge them, just too heavy I guess.

The Monkey Man walked over to the closest jar and ran the detector up and down it from all sides. "Not a damn thing" he said.

"What if it's lined with lead?" Said Cyrano.

"It would pick up the lead" said The Monkey Man.

"Damn" said Cyrano, "you mean to tell me I came all the way out hear for nothin'."

"Looks like" said The Monkey Man.

"What ya say we just blow one of these things up with a little C-4" said Cyrano.

"It'd just be a waste of time" said The Monkey Man.

"I ain't even believin' this shit" said Cyrano.

The Monkey Man tried several more of the jars and had swept most of the area with his machine when Fingers called out "looks like we've got some company."

They were being approached by a squad of Rangers led by a full bird colonel who did not appear to be in a good mood as he yelled out "Do you idiots realize that you just gave away our position!"

"Sorry sir" said The Monkey Man, "but we've got orders for you from higher up and since your radios appear to be out, this is the only way we could get through to you."

"Well thank God for that anyway" said the Colonel. "This has got be the strangest mission I've ever been on. First our radios all go out at the same time and then instead of observing NVA troop movements we end up watching some sort of weird religious ceremony. Come on we'd better get out of this place before they show up again. It won't be long before dark and that seems to be their time."

The Monkey Man and his crew followed the Colonel back to his position a short distance away on the far side of a small ridge line.

"So what are the orders from higher up?" Said the Colonel.

"They want you to attack the enemy position tonight" said The Monkey Man.

"Attack?" Said the Colonel. "The only weapons these guys have are bamboo knives, we'd slaughter them!"

"In that case," said The Monkey Man, "I guess you'll just have to capture them. Here," he said handing the Ranger Colonel a radio,

"This was working just a few minutes ago and hopefully it still is, check it out for yourself."

The Ranger Colonel called Long Tieng and confirmed the order. He also set a time and location for a pick-up zone the next day assuming the radio would meet the same fate as the others shortly after dark.

The Colonel quickly called a CP meeting with his officers making plans for the attack. When he was finished a few minutes later he turned to The Monkey Man and asked "So can you tell us what the hell is going on around here?"

The Monkey Man quickly answered back "we were hoping you'd be able to tell us. All intelligence knows so far is that for some unknown reason after dark in this area radios don't work, compasses spin like tops, bombs don't explode and aircraft engines don't work. The radios being permanently destroyed is the latest development. Who knows what'll happen next? So tell me colonel," said The Monkey Man, "what exactly did you guys see last night?"

"Well," said the Ranger Colonel, "we got into position before dark as ordered. We really had no idea of what we were up against but we expected to find heavy enemy resistance on the way in. Instead we were totally unopposed. There was not a sign of any enemy activity on the way. We considered ourselves damn lucky to make it without being detected. Our objective, the area surrounding the jars, was totally deserted as it is now. Our orders were to observe and send back any information we could. We sent out a negative situation report just before dark. Then the sun went down along with all of our radios. The strangest thing I've ever seen, totally unheard of."

"It was completely quiet then for quite some time, with no sign of the enemy, when suddenly from a distance came one of the strangest sounds I've ever heard. Our first thought was of dinosaurs believe it or not. I mean what with the way this land looks, so primitive and all, downright prehistoric. The ground started shaking and we figured if it's not dinosaurs then it must be NVA tanks. I don't know which would have been worse!"

"A short time later they finally appeared from over a rise in the land. It looked like something right out of the history books, Hannibal's army! Turns out what we thought were dinosaurs were really elephants. We'd heard the NVA used them but none of us had ever seen one over here. Our orders were just to observe, not to make contact, and since our radios were down we couldn't call in an air strike anyway so we just sat tight and waited."

"When they got close up to the jars we were in for another surprise. They weren't NVA or Chinese, they weren't Meo or the Laotian Army, and they weren't even armed with any sort of modern weapons. They looked like something out of the distant past. They wore primitive clothing and the only weapons they carried were bamboo knives and spears."

"They looked as though they were here to throw a party. Then they built this huge bonfire with wood they'd brought with them and cooked a huge meal over the fire, the smell was fantastic. It made us all hungry. After they ate they started passing pipes, those bong things, ya no, and what must have been rice wine around the fire."

"They started laughin' and jokin'. They were havin' a great old time. They had women with 'em too, and the women got up and started to dance around the fire. Great lookin' women too. I tell ya it was everything we could do to keep from joining them. It really looked just too good to be true. We figured it must have been some sort of a trap. A damn strange trap though. I mean who would go to all that trouble in a place like this, out in the middle of nowhere?"

Hoang had been listening quietly to the Ranger Colonel as he spoke. "Spirits!" Hoang said. "What you speak of are spirits of our ancestors. I have heard stories like this. We must not treat them with disrespect. They posses great power, more than your greatest weapons. They don't fear death because they already dead. There must be some purpose for their appearance. They do not let themselves be seen by us, let alone strangers such as yourselves from other countries. I think that something very important will happen here."

"Be that as it may" said the Ranger Colonel with a look of doubt on his face. "After a considerable amount of partying they formed another circle around two of the young men. It looked as though they were going to have some sort of contest. The contest turned out to be a knife fight using their bamboo knives. They both appeared to be quite good fighters. The fight turned out to be to the death and went on for quite some time. Towards the end it became a rather gruesome affair until one of the boys finally weakened and died from several wounds. The winner of the fight was treated as a hero. He was taken away by a group of the young women who bandaged his wounds, and took care of him in other ways too."

"If these guys are already dead," said Cyrano to Hoang, "how come one of them died?" Hoang just shrugged his shoulders.

"Because we were afraid this was some sort of a trap," the Ranger Colonel continued, "we decided to send out several listening posts around the area. They came back in this morning with reports of no NVA sightings.

The sun had set while the Ranger Colonel spoke and it was quickly becoming dark. The Colonel nodded to The Monkey Man. "Try that radio again." The Monkey Man pushed the send bar on the radio expecting the normal hissing sound of white noise. He got nothing, the radio was dead like the others. "Damn" said the Ranger Colonel. "This place is beginning to look like a bad dream."

Now the ground began to shake. In the distance a loud cry was heard. "Sounds like Tyrannosaurus Rex to me" said Doc.

"No shit" said Cyrano. They all watched in amazement as the ancient past seemed to be revealing itself before their eyes. "The Kingdom of Lan Xang, the land of a million elephants" said Cyrano.

Hoang looked on nervously.

The scene was a repeat of the night before. "Say Colonel," said The Monkey Man. "You sendin' out LPs (listening posts) tonight?"

"Not without radios" said the Colonel. "They won't do us any good tonight unless we can communicate with them. I don't want to take a chance of accidentally shooting them up like we almost did when they came in this morning."

"I'd like to know what's happening on the other side of that party." said The Monkey Man.

"You and me both" said the Ranger Colonel.

The party slowly played itself out. The men watching, including Cyrano and Doc, wished they could join in. They looked as though they were having a great time. The only man among them who didn't want anything to do with the party was Hoang. He wanted nothing to do with them and only wished he could be back with his friends where he belonged.

"We'll wait 'til the knife fight begins" said the Ranger Colonel. "That's when they're the most distracted. Then we'll go in quietly and surround them. Since they appear to be unarmed I don't want any shots fired. We don't want another My Lai on our hands, especially out here. We'll just walk in on them, check out their operation and search everything. We'll capture their leaders and any suspicious looking equipment they have. Then we'll hold them there 'til sunrise, wait for our extraction birds and fly them back for higher higher to check out. We'll be out of here in no time."

"Sounds like a piece of cake" said The Monkey Man.

"Yea" said the Ranger Colonel, "just like every other operation I've been on. They all sound like a piece of cake until you try to carry them out!"

The Rangers watched the tribe carry on for what seemed like an eternity. Their stomachs growled at the smell of roasting meat in the air, cooked over an open fire. An open fire they thought, what a luxury that would be. The Rangers soaked their dehydrated lurp rations in water until they were soft enough to eat. No fires or noise were allowed because it would give away their position.

Finally the old tribe began to form a circle for the knife fight. Just like the night before using one of the jars as the center of the circle. The Rangers slowly and quietly began to move out. Normally they would have left a command post in place with the Colonel and maybe half the men. But with no radios and no way to communicate with his men the Colonel decided it would be best for them to stay within shouting distance.

They split into two columns when they got within two hundred yards of the tribe, each column went in the opposite direction. Very slowly and very quietly they made their way into a semicircle around the camp. The Knife fight was ferocious and the crowd ooh'ed and ahh'ed with each slash of the bamboo knives helping the Rangers to stay undetected.

The fight came to a sudden end when one of the competitors managed to slash the jugular vein of his foe before the Rangers were in position. But the Rangers kept moving as the winner of the fight was carried off for his just rewards.

The loser of the fight became the focus point of another ceremony, his blood was drained and passed to a circle of old men sitting cross-legged around the victim. Each of the old men took a sip of the blood and passed it on. When the blood had been consumed the victim's body was ceremonially placed into the jar which had been the center of the fighting circle.

The Ranger Colonel, hoping that all of his men had had time to get into position, gave a hand signal to the man on each side of him. He waited until he thought his men had all received the signal passed down the columns and then began moving toward the tribe.

Just as he began his move he heard a metallic click, the sound of a firing pin striking home on the shell casing of a bullet. He instinctively hit the ground just as a call came out from behind him "NVA!"

The colonel had ordered half of his men to face in the opposite direction and to stay in place as perimeter security. One of them had just sighted a large column of NVA approaching their perimeter. The soldier had fired upon them but his rifle had misfired and jammed so he yelled out as a warning to the rest of the men.

After the scream both the NVA and the Rangers aimed their rifles at each other and pulled the triggers. Instead of the deafening sound of automatic weapons fire all that was heard was the sound of hundreds of firing pins hitting brass, followed by a lot of cussing and the metallic sound of bolts being pulled back to eject a dead round, then more clicks.

Finally there was total silence as the men on both sides wondered what was going on. God damn, the Colonel thought to himself. I had a feeling something like this was going to happen, spirits of the dead ha!

Slowly, from somewhere behind him laughter began to build. He looked around and saw that at first the old men, and then the rest of the tribe of spirits, or whatever they were, were laughing. The laughter became louder and louder until it got to the point where it drowned out the Colonel's own thoughts. Almost as a defense against the laughter the Ranger Colonel yelled "fix bayonets!" The laughter slowly began to subside, replaced by the metallic sound of hundreds of bayonets being attached to rifles, then silence for a few, slow seconds, and finally the order "Charge!"

The roar of the men's screams was bone chilling as they ran toward the NVA. Still screaming as they ran, just like they had been taught in training. It was automatic to them now. They did not have to think of what they were doing. Their bodies moved faster than conscious thought would allow. The adrenaline began pumping and the survival instinct took over.

As Fingers and The Monkey Man joined the charge they yelled back to their troops "Stay here, stay here until you're called for.

Hoang you guard them as they work." Then they disappeared into the melee.

Doc sat watching, waiting for the cry of "Medic!" when he felt a presence directly behind him. Out of reflex action caused by fear for his life Doc turned around and faced the presence. It was one of the old Shamans from the tribe. The old man spoke to Doc in a language he could not know yet somehow seemed to understand. The language must have been very old for the sounds were of a mixture of grunts and gasps.

Cyrano and Hoang also heard the sounds the Shaman was making and turned around. They both instinctively pointed their bayoneted weapons at him and them stared almost in shock. Hoang then through his rifle down to the ground in front of him, knelt and bowed face to the ground before the old man. Cyrano just stared. The old man took a leather-like pouch from around his neck and placed it around Doc's neck.

Doc opened the pouch and looked in. It was filled with a black liquid. He stuck the tip of one finger in and touched the liquid goo, then brought the finger to his nose and sniffed it. "Liquid opium" he said out loud.

"Medic!" The three of them turned at once and began to run in the direction of the call. The screams and the moans of the wounded could be heard above the sounds of the battle. Even without gunfire war was loud.

They came upon the first wounded man. Doc was surprised at the severity of the wounds. The man looked as though he had been torn apart by shrapnel. "God damn" said Cyrano. "I guess it doesn't matter what they use for weapons. The results seem to be the same."

"Yea" said Doc as he gently secured the wounded man's intestines to his slit open belly with a field dressing. The wounded soldier began to scream out in pain realizing what had happened to him.

"Hey Cyrano" cried Doc. "You got a fit kit on ya."

"Yea" said Cyrano. "I was just thinkin' the same thought, we're out of morphine but that liquid opium you've got will work just as good, I've used it before." As Cyrano prepared the injection he heard the sound of metal on metal behind him. He didn't bother to look, he was too busy and had a great deal of faith in Hoang and Doc. Doc looked up and grabbed his bayoneted M16. He was just in time to see Hoang pull his machete out of a soldiers chest and then with the same motion slit another's throat. Doc looked around, there was a lot of fighting going on but their immediate area looked safe.

Two minutes later the young ranger with the slit open stomach had stopped screaming and seemed to be in a very relaxed mood. Doc felt his pulse and it seemed strong enough. He handed the man his rifle and told him to relax. "Don't worry man, you're goin' back to the world."

"Medic!" Doc, Cyrano and Hoang moved on, there was much work to be done. The night was almost over and the sky was starting to lighten. As Doc looked around him he began to notice the size of the dead NVA strewn around him, they were big NVA. Hoang was the first to say it. "Chinese" he said "they're Chinese." Doc wasn't really surprised, after all he had been in Laos once before with the Cav. It hadn't been that long ago, not more than two months but it seemed like a life time ago. The Cav had seen the Chinese before but they had run away, back to the border where they had artillery support. Orders from higher up. The Rangers weren't taking any orders from anyone but themselves. They couldn't. Their radios were dead.

The battle was slowing down, the Rangers were winning but at a price, there were a great number of wounded. They had their own medics with them and they were all working as hard as Doc and Cyrano.

The tribe, which was somehow causing the weapons to misfire, left as they did each night before sunrise at which time things went back to normal except for the batteries in the radios which had lost their charge.

The sun finally rose over a far off mountain range and with it came another strange sight. Old prop driven airplanes, a lot of them. It looked like a sight from World War Two as they dove in on the melee. They opened up with their machine guns firing over everyone's heads. The Chinese instantly broke contact with the Rangers and began running for their lives. It was a mistake. They were gunned down by the diving aircraft. The Rangers discovering their weapons were working again opened up on the stragglers. The battle had quickly turned into a massacre. The few Chinese who were left refused to surrender and fired back at the Rangers who quickly finished them off.

In the heat of the battle the tribe had been forgotten. When the men finally looked for them no one was surprised at the fact that they were gone.

As Cyrano worked on one of the wounded men he noticed the dead Chinese soldier laying next to him. The Chinese soldier had been weighed down by a very heavy ruck sack which had somehow been slit open. There was a pile of fine powder on the ground next to the ruck. That powder looked familiar to Cyrano. He reached over and took a small taste of the powder. "Wow" he said out loud, "pure heroin." Cyrano opened up the dead man's pack and looked inside. "Man, I ain't even believin' this!" There was at least twenty pounds of heroin in the ruck sack. Cyrano looked around to make sure no one was looking and quickly stuffed as much of it as he could fit into his own ruck sack.

He looked around again and noticed that all the Chinese soldiers had very well filled ruck sacks. He went over to another fallen soldier and checked his pack, it also had a good twenty pounds of smack in it, "Holy shit!"

Chapter 11
JOLLY GREEN T-REX

The battle was over and the Rangers had won decisively. No prisoners had been taken because they had all refused to surrender and only a few of them had managed to escape. The Ranger Colonel was proud of his men, his only disappointment was the fact that the tribe had somehow managed to escape in the confusion of the battle. That tribe he thought was one strange group. They weren't Hmong and they weren't Montagnard. He had no idea what they were and wondered if they really had anything to do with the dead radios or the weapons that wouldn't fire. Curious he thought, and figured now he never would find out. He hoped maybe those Air Force planes would find out. And another thing, what were we doing fighting with old Korean War vintage prop driven aircraft. Jeese what the hell is going on here?

When the Ranger Colonel finally ordered his men to search the dead Chinese bodies he discovered the biggest surprise of all, heroin! Not just a few small vials of the stuff which was not uncommon, but instead they found unbelievable quantities of the stuff, hundreds of pounds. There was only one explanation for this much being transported. The Chinese soldiers had been heading east to Vietnam. The heroin had to be headed for American soldiers. They were the only ones with enough money for this unbelievable quantity. The Chinese and the NVA had to be working together on this one. One more way to wear down the American will to fight, the Colonel thought, God what a way to fight a war!

The Colonel ordered his men to stack it all into one large pile. When they had finished the Ranger Colonel took a burning torch and lit the kindling which had been placed beneath the heroin. In a few minutes the pile of heroin was ablaze.

The Ranger Colonel said to The Monkey Man, "I realize that according to procedure I should have called this in before I took any action but since we didn't have any radios I guess I didn't have any choice."

"Yea," said The Monkey Man, "higher would have brought the stuff back in for analysis and evidence. But we both know damn well how that would have worked."

"It would have found its way right back into the hands of the people it was headed for in the first place" said the Ranger Colonel.

"Yea," said The Monkey Man, "and we would have had even more of our men strung out on the stuff than we already do."

"Hell of a rotten way to fight a war" said the Ranger Colonel.

The body count was finished just before the choppers began to arrive at their predetermined time. The wounded were loaded aboard the first choppers followed by the Ranger dead. The Chinese were left where they lay. As the last of the choppers came in the black helicopter appeared on the horizon. It waited until the last Ranger chopper had left before it landed. Fingers, The Monkey Man, Doc, Cyrano and Hoang had all survived the ordeal without a scratch.

They were all glad to leave but they were still curious about the strange tribe people, all but Hoang that is for he already knew the legend of the Tribe of the Jars. The Monkey Man ordered the chopper pilot to follow the trail left by the elephants. He then turned to Hoang. "Where do you think they're headed?"

"They're spirits" said Hoang. "They go where they want. They will not let us catch them unless they want. They can disappear. As I say before they have more power than your nuclear bombs. We should not try to follow them."

The chopper flew low to the ground following the well defined trail left by the elephants. The trail came to a river, the tracks led in on one side but on the other there was nothing, not a sign of the heavy beasts. The chopper pilot looked at The Monkey Man. "Take a left" said the Monkey 'Man. "I think I know where their headed, south to the secret city."

They followed the river for some distance watching for tracks along the banks but there was no sign of anything. "I don't think they could have got this far" said Fingers.

"Yea," said The Monkey Man, "it's beginning to look hopeless."

Just then the pilot noticed several smoky fires burning on a mountain side in front of them far off in the distance. "Planes down!" He yelled back to the rest of them.

The black chopper approached the burning wrecks cautiously expecting enemy fire from the ground, when there was a blinding flash followed by what appeared to be a huge rocket ascending straight into the sky and quickly disappearing from sight. "What the fuck was that?" Yelled Fingers.

"I don't know" said The Monkey Man, "but since we sure as hell can't follow it let's find out where it came from." As they flew by the burning aircraft they could see no survivors. Close to the top of the mountain ridge though they saw one of the old prop fighter planes.

It had managed to land on its belly. It looked like it had skidded a short distance up the mountain before coming to rest just before reaching the top. "They must have lost power again" said the Monkey Man.

"That must have been some pilot to land that plane" said the chopper pilot.

As the chopper moved in closer they could see the pilot. He was sitting on the ground staring straight ahead up the mountain to a small but level spot on the peak. The spot he was staring at must have been where the flash of blinding white light had come from because there was a large black circle there. The rock looked as though it had been melted, and parts of it were still glowing red as the chopper landed nearby to pick up the downed pilot. Doc and The Monkey Man both got out of the helicopter to help the pilot who hadn't even seemed to notice the chopper, he was still staring at the black spot. As they ran down to him they could feel the intense heat coming off that spot. Doc looked at it as he ran by. It seemed as though the rock had been turned to glass just like the pictures he'd seen of nuclear bomb tests. It was an awesome sight.

When they got to the pilot he still had not moved his gaze from that black spot. The man looked as though he was in some sort of a trance. Doc asked him if he was OK but got no reply. He waved his hand in front of the man's face, still nothing. The pilots pupils were dilated and they did not react to motion. Finally The Monkey Man slapped him across the face, this seemed to bring him out of it just long enough to say a few words "T-Rex, I just saw a god damn dinosaur" and then the man went back into his trance, still staring straight ahead.

The sound of another chopper approaching made both Doc and The Monkey Man jump in sudden fear. As the chopper came into view over the ridge of the mountain they almost expected to see Tyrannosaurus Rex's gaping jaws and huge teeth. They were relieved to see it was just another American chopper. It was a strange looking bird though, a model Doc had never seen before.

"Air America's Jolly Green to the rescue" said The Monkey Man. "I can't believe it took them this long to get here. They must be having radio problems too." The Jolly Green set down next to the black chopper. Several of the crew members got out. At the same time Fingers, Cyrano and Hoang got out to help as well.

Fingers ran over and said "Hi" to the Jolly Green's crew members. He obviously had met them before. They carried on like old friends that hadn't seen each other for a while as they made their way down the steep slope to the downed planes. "Uh oh, The Monkey Man's loose again" one of them yelled out.

Cyrano helped the pilot who was still alive into the big Air America chopper where two Air Force medics tried to bring the pilot back to reality. They didn't have much luck.

Everyone but one of the Air Force medics and the surviving pilot pitched in to extract the bodies of the dead pilots from their wrecked and now smoldering planes. It was a messy job and several of the men had to take time out. The occasional man suddenly turned very pale, quickly turned to stumble away from the plane and rather embarrassingly lose his lunch. It seemed to be contagious.

When all of the body parts were neatly zippered up into body bags they were carried up to the waiting Jolly Green which then quickly lifted up and flew down the other side of the mountain.

Doc was standing next to The Monkey Man as they all watched the chopper descend into the valley and for the first time Doc and Cyrano noticed there was a huge city down there. A huge city with an air field full of old fighter planes and new helicopters.

"Holly shit!" Said Doc, "what's that?"

"That's Long Tieng!" Said The Monkey Man, "the secret city. Uh, just pretend you didn't see it man. And that's an order!"

"Right," said Doc, "and speaking of seeing things what do you think that poor pilot saw that freaked him out so bad? That mumbling about Tyrannosaurus Rex was freakin' *me* out."

"That's a weird one all right" said The Monkey Man. "but you've got to figure that man just watched his best buddies die right before his eyes. Watching your friends die like that can make anybody a little strange."

"Yea, I know" said Doc.

"There's one more thing though" said The Monkey Man. "Those Air America boys said they were slow in getting here because they were having radio problems. As a matter of fact they said every radio in the Secret City went out at the same time."

"Yea" added Cyrano, "and what the hell was that huge rocket thing we saw just before we got here. I'd be willing to bet it came right from that black spot there and it's damn obvious that's right where these planes were headed. Whatever it was, the pilots thought it was their target."

"I don't know.' said The Monkey Man, "This is the strangest shit I've ever run up against. One thing for sure though. We've got to get the hell out of this place before anything else happens. We did everything we could and as far as I'm concerned our mission is over, at least for now. Come on let's get back to the Ranch and have a beer."

"There it is!" Said Fingers. They all hopped aboard the chopper and flew back down the mountain and away from Long Tieng the Secret City.

They flew low across the Plain of Jars heading for the ridge of mountains on the far side. There a small Green Beret and Hmong outpost guarded the high plain from an almost constant invading force of the North Vietnamese government. These invasions were supported by Russia and China despite the fact that China did not usually get along very well with either Russia or North Vietnam. It was a complicated situation made even more so by the American involvement. The Secret City of Long Tieng was no secret to the Chinese government, and it may well have been the reason for their involvement in the war. The fact was they actually feared the

Americans might try to invade them! It may have seemed like paranoia from the American point of view but China feared the awesome high tech military industrial complex of the most powerful government on earth.

The Ranch was just one of many small outposts of Hmong soldiers which had been supported by the US since the French were defeated in the fifties. When President Kennedy created the Green Beret Special Forces in the early Sixties Laos became one of their first areas of operation under the code name of White Star mobile training teams. Small groups of highly trained Green Berets traveled among the Hmong tribes bringing them weapons, food and medical assistance in exchange for their support against the Communists.

The Secret City was their headquarters. They provided their own air support, using old American military airplanes flown by Hmong, US Air Force and the CIA's Air America pilots and had more air support available from the Air Force with planes stationed at bases in nearby Thailand. The Secret City was also the headquarters of General Vang Poe, the strong and resourceful military leader of the Hmong people. His military exploits had already reached the status of legend among his people.

CHAPTER 12
Beer, Steaks, And A Ten Thousand Dollar Question

The Monkey Man and his crew pulled up to the Ranch without the excitement that he'd created the last time he'd come in, no doubt only because this time he wasn't at the controls.

The Special Forces Captain was waiting for him at the chopper pad as they landed. He saluted The Monkey Man as he jumped out of the chopper. "Well done men, mission accomplished. I knew if anyone could pull it off it would be you. I've already heard from the Rangers and they were damn excited about this operation's outcome. We knew something big had to be going on down there on the plain what with all that radio jamming going on but we had no idea it was anything this big. The Ranger Colonel told me you guys must have burned close to one thousand pounds of pure uncut heroin. We've been trying to find out for over a year now where that stuff was coming from. Those god damn Chinese, we've got more GIs on heroin here than there are junkies in New York City."

"Hey Monkey Man" said Doc, "we're gonna go explore the base and grab a bite to eat, it's almost lunch time."

"Go ahead" said The Monkey Man, "just make sure you're back here in two hours, we've got to get you guys back to your jeep at the Rock Pile. And hey you guys did a real good job out there. You all deserve bronze stars for that, but since this is a top secret operation I'm afraid we can't give 'em to ya. You'll be paid real good for the whores though and you can buy more with money than you can with a bronze star."

"Right on!" Said Cyrano.

The mess hall wouldn't open for another half hour so Doc, Cyrano and Hoang set off to explore the Hmong and Special Forces base.

A small Cessna was landing at the air strip so they wandered over to take a look. The pilot that finally emerged from the cockpit looked to be in his mid fifties, with dark hair that was graying around the edges. He was dressed in a brightly colored Hawaiian sport shirt. Doc and Cyrano thought he looked like a rich tourist with his own airplane. He would have looked out of place across the border in Vietnam, but in this strange land he seemed to fit right in.

The pilot looked at Hoang as though he recognized him and then yelled out in a heavy French accent "Hoang what are you doing hear?"

"Pierre" Hoang cried out as they hugged each other.

Pierre slapped Hoang on the back and said "You're looking good. You've really filled out since the last time I saw you back at Mai Loc. You look just like your dad when he was your age." Hoang had tears in his eyes now. Seeing this old friend of his father reminded him of happier times many years ago. It seemed to Hoang like a lifetime ago.

"I haven't seen your dad in four or five years, how the hell is the old soldier."

Hoang looked away and with a barely audible voice he said "he's dead."

"I'm sorry Hoang. Damn it's hard to believe after all the things that man survived. We fought together against the Japanese back in World war two. Now that was a war, back then we knew what we were fighting for and who the enemy was. Now days everything seems confused. I can't tell who's fighting for what anymore. Shit, most people don't even care. I just do my job and fuck the rest of it. There's just too many politicians in the world these days."

"How's the rest of the family Hoang, your mom OK?"

"They're fine" said Hoang.

"God she's one hell of a woman but I'll bet she took it hard. I'll have to stop down and pay my respects, damn hard to believe after all he went through."

"Say who's yer American buddies here?" Hoang introduced Doc and Cyrano. They listened to the Frenchman tell old war stories as the Hmong tribesmen who gathered around began unloading guns and ammunition from the plane.

When the Hmong had finished unloading the ammo they began loading the plane back up with sticky bricks of raw opium. "Holy shit" said Cyrano, "look at all that opium, Jesus, what the hell is going on hear?"

"Settle down there young man. I realize this may look strange to you but you've got to understand the complexity of the situation here. The Hmong have been growing opium in these mountains for generations, it's the only cash crop they can grow in the area and they've got just as much right to earn a living as any of us."

"Don't get me wrong" said Cyrano. "I've got nothing against smokin' a little O every now and then, or even snortin' a little smack on occasion. It's just that I didn't expect to see this stuff going on right under the noses of the CIA and the US military, I mean isn't it illegal or something."

"I'm afraid war makes it's own laws" said the old Frenchman. "But I know your military people are very much against this. The fact is they have no choice but to let it continue. They are forced to look the other way because of the unpopular nature of the war back in the states. The CIA does not have the money to support the Hmong Army so they must let them support themselves, and growing opium in these mountains is the only way the Hmong know. They're good at it, they have been doing this for a long time. When my country was fighting this war we did the same thing. Things have not changed much here since the Americans took over the war."

"People back in the world have no idea any of this is even going on" said Cyrano. "Shit we've got soldiers dying every day in Vietnam and most of the people back in the world don't even care about that. They just go about their lives worrying about the latest fashion trends while we're fuckin' dyin' over here. They don't care man, they don't even fuckin' care!"

"Hey you guys" said the old Frenchman, "I care, I've been caring about these people for a lot of years. I've grown to love them over the years, although sometimes I really wonder if we're doing any good here. Maybe we should just get out and let them solve their problems on their own. All we've really done here is to teach them how to kill each other more efficiently with our modern war machines. Maybe their old ways were better. No matter, I guess it's too late now with the Russians and Americans using the country as a test ground for their latest weapons."

"If we could have spent the money on food, medical supplies and modern farming equipment both sides could have saved a lot of money, but more importantly the people would be a lot better off. Hell, who am I to speak when they've got a REMF like Henry Kissinger making the decisions over here!"

"Uh yea" said Cyrano. "Say ah, who is it you work for anyway?"

"The Company of course, Air America. You might say that I'm just sort of free lancing for them. Some people call us mercenaries or soldiers of fortune but I don't care much for those names myself. They remind me too much of my old job back when I was a young man like you guys."

"And what job was that?" Asked Doc.

"The French Foreign Legion."

"Somehow I guess we should have known that" said Cyrano.

"Far out! Said Doc.

"Speaking of far out" said the old Frenchman. "I've got to be on my way. And hey Hoang, tell your mother I'll be paying her a visit for the Tet holiday and I expect to see you there. You're wandering a bit far from home you know. You're just like your father was when he was your age. I'll see you for Tet Hoang. Nice meeting you boys and don't let Hoang here get into any trouble."

The old Frenchman, his plane loaded with opium, revved his engine building up power for his take off from the short landing strip on top of the mountain. When he released the brake the plane suddenly catapulted down the runway. It was so loaded down that it actually sunk down out of view at the end of the runway using an updraft from the mountain to finally gain altitude.

"I wonder where he takes all stuff to" said Cyrano.

"There's a ten thousand dollar Question for ya." said Doc.

"Hell of a lot more than that I'll bet" said Cyrano.

"Yea, no shit" said Doc.

Hoang, Doc and Cyrano headed for the mess hall still wondering.

The mess hall wasn't much even by Dong Ha standards, just an army issue canvas tent. The food was served out of standard issue mermack cans. Dehydrated potatoes and shit on a shingle once again. "God I'd give my soul for a cheeseburger" said Cyrano.

"I don't think you've even got a soul" said Doc.

"Ah spirits!" Said Hoang and all three of them broke out laughing remembering the strange tribe at the Jars.

There was an odd mix of men in the tent, mainly Hmong soldiers or Meo as everybody called them, General Vang Pao's boys. A few Air Force guys, some Green Berets and a hand full of the Company men dressed mainly in what seemed to be their CIA issue Hawaiian sport shirts. "Jesus Christ, look what the cat dragged in" yelled out one of the Hawaiian shirts.

Everybody turned toward the door just in time to see Fingers and The Monkey Man come through the door with a cooler of beer. They yelled out in unison "Fix bayonets. Charge!" They ran to the table chanting "Airborne Ranger, Green Beret, all the way!" And slammed the cooler of beer down in front of Hoang.

"Ah, the spirits of war" said Cyrano.

"It's party time" yelled The Monkey Man as he pulled about twenty steaks from the huge ice chest and through them to the cook.

"Steaks, beer and ice," yelled out one of the Hawaiian shirts, "Jesus Christ, we must be in heaven, where in the hell did you get that stuff from?"

Fingers plunked down a large cassette tape player in the middle of the table and pushed down the play button. The song "Born To Be Wild" by Steppenwolf filled the tent as the men grabbed for the cold beer. Hoang's girlfriend Tray and the two prostitutes came in and started dancing to the wild music using a few pushed together tables as a stage.

Many war stories were told, some even of dinosaurs, of UFO's and the ancient tribe who may have left the jars on the plain. Many stories told, but few believed. Spirits and ghosts have been soldiers' companions throughout history, it's the nature of their work.

A good time was had by all. At least until the beer ran out an hour later. After all there was a war going on, jobs to be done and guard duty to be pulled that night. As The Monkey Man put it, "relaxing is good for the soul, but only in moderation if the soul is to be kept with the body."

"Well troops" The Monkey Man said to Hoang, Cyrano and Doc, "I believe part of our deal was to get you guys back to the Rock Pile this afternoon, so I guess we better get a move on."

"What about the other part of the deal?" Said Cyrano.

"Oh yea, the money, I thought you'd never ask. Fingers, pay the man."

Fingers reached into his pocket and laid down ten slightly worn one hundred dollar bills on the table in front of Cyrano. "Cheapest helicopter I've ever bought" he said.

"Well you guys drive a hard bargain" said Cyrano. "Besides my overhead was pretty low on this one."

"Let's move out troops" The Monkey Man said as he headed for the door. They loaded their gear minus most of the ammunition. Fingers said it was part of "the deal and besides the choppers too heavy already." Cyrano didn't complain, he didn't feel like carrying it anyway. The women hopped in, they were laughing and giggling again after the excitement of the party. Fingers gave the two pilots the thumbs up sign and yelled "Sky!" The chopper lifted up from the mountain top Hmong outpost and headed east under a clear sky with the sun still high and a little behind them in the west.

"Keep your eyes open for NVA" The Monkey Man yelled out. "There should be a company or two of them headed this way looking for those Chinese dudes we wiped out this morning."

The chopper flew a zig-zag pattern close to the ground looking for any signs of enemy traffic. The Plain of Jars looked deserted, there was no sign of any kind of human activity. They passed over the jars they had spent the night before observing, and then the battlefield. The bodies were still strewn about where they had fallen. They were starting to bloat now in the afternoon sun. Giant black birds were feasting on their remains.

"Doesn't look like anybody's going to bury them" said The Monkey Man.

"No" said Fingers. "It might take a week for the Chinese to send another patrol down here from where they're working on that new road in northern Laos, near the Chinese border. Ya know, I hear they've got thirty thousand troops working on that road now. A lot of men just for doin' some road work."

"Yea," said The Monkey Man, "and ya know damn well the NVA won't bury the poor bastards."

"No way" said Fingers. "Those guys hate each other. I can't believe they're working together on this dope deal. They really must want us out'a here bad. Not a good sign. I wonder how much longer the Ranch can hold out?"

"Not long" said The Monkey Man. "But what I'm worried about is Long Tieng and General Vang Pao. If the Chinese and NVA work together they'll be able to take that place at will. Vang Pao may be able to escape but eventually they'll hunt him down."

"Yea" said Fingers, "when they get Vang Pao they've got the country and that means our asses are out'a here, and maybe out'a Vietnam too. If the Chinese and NVA can use Laos and the Ho Chi Minh Trail as a staging area unopposed we're in big trouble."

"Yea," said The Monkey Man, "it could happen."

The chopper searched for hours on its way back to the Rock Pile without a sign of the NVA below them. "Let's see how close we can get to the Rock this time" said Fingers to the chopper pilot.

"You know they've got SAMs (surface to air missiles) up there now" said the pilot.

"Ah don't worry about it" said Fingers. "They're not gonna waste SAMs on just one little chopper, they're savin' 'em for the zoomies (jet planes)."

The chopper pilot started to make a long arch around the lone mountain peak. "Hey," said Doc "look at all the flowers they've got growing up there."

"Yea" said Cyrano, "poppies, they're growin' opium up there!" Suddenly the mountain top erupted with anti-aircraft machine gun fire. Two of the rounds some how managed to bounce off the tail of the chopper even from the distance they were at, one that the pilot thought would be out of range.

"Jesus," said The Monkey Man, "they must have some new Russian guns up there too. Let's get the hell outta here before they decide to try out one of those SAMs after all." The chopper pilot appeared to agree wholeheartedly as he quickly switched directions and headed back towards South Vietnam and the Rock Pile.

"It's a waste of fuckin' time hunting for NVA in broad daylight" said Fingers.

"Yea," said The Monkey Man, "these damn slicks make too much noise. We'll just have to wait for the Raven FACs to find them."

Fingers yelled out to the chopper pilot, "we'd better get these kids back home before dark." Still flying close to the ground the helicopter stopped its wandering and headed straight in the direction of the Rock Pile.

Chapter 13
Thousand Yard Stare Or-Gratefully Dead

A few hours later, close to dinner time they came in for a landing at what was left of the Rock Pile. The Cav was still there guarding the base. Their Tracks and Sheridan Tanks had the perimeter surrounded.

Choppers and truck convoys had been coming in all day with men and supplies. The new men were easy to distinguish from the survivors of the battle two nights ago. Most of the replacements appeared to be FNGs (Fucking New Guys) in bright green new uniforms. The veterans' uniforms were faded and permeated with the red dust which was so prevalent in the area. The effect was a sort of natural camouflage, so they blended right in with the surrounding hill sides.

But the thing which really set them apart was their eyes. The new guys had nervous eyes which darted from place to place while the old timers had a relaxed tiredness to their stares almost like they were too tired to care anymore. Often they would stare straight ahead with unfocused eyes looking at nothing. The thousand yard stare!

Doc noticed this as they got off the chopper and it brought to mind the name of a popular band at the time, the Grateful Dead.

As the Monkey Man got off the chopper he was greeted by Captain Black, the CO of the Cav Troop. "I want to thank you for what you guys did the other night" he said. "You saved our asses on that mountain side. I don't think we would have made it without you."

"Yea," said The Monkey Man, "they had you guys pinned down pretty good. I can't believe you tried to make that climb at night without any air support. I don't even think John Wayne would have tried that one."

"Well," said the Captain "We had to save the Rock Pile, we've got to look out for our own men you know."

"Yea, I know" said The Monkey Man. "I guess we were both a little lucky. I just wish we could say the same for most of the men here that night."

"At least we managed to save some of our boys," said the Captain, "too bad about Colonel Travis though. Sort of ironic with that name and all."

"He was a good soldier" said The Monkey Man.

"Yes he was." said the Captain, "Well, we'll be heading back to Dong Ha to finish our stand down in a couple of hours, but until then we've got hot chow and cold beer for everyone."

"I wish we could oblige you," said The Monkey Man "but we've got to get back to the Ranch before night fall, there's been a lot of enemy activity in our area and we don't want the same thing to happen there."

"Thanks again and good luck" said Captain Black.

As The Monkey Man climbed back into his chopper he waved good-bye to his troops and yelled out "Be cool and keep your powder dry. Hoang don't forget I'll meet you at Mai Loc in three days." The chopper quickly climbed into the sky and headed back to the Great Northwest Territory.

"Those guys are nuts" said the Captain as he watched the chopper fly off.

"No shit" said Doc.

"Captain," said Cyrano, "do you mind if we pull our jeep into your formation for the trip back to Dong Ha?"

"Don't mind at all" said the Captain. "We owe you guys, if there's anything you need just let me know."

"Thanks" said Cyrano. "Come on guys and girls, let's have some dinner before we have to hit the road again."

Hoang, Doc, Cyrano and the girls dropped off what little equipment they had left at the jeep which appeared to be OK except for a few shrapnel dents and bullet holes. Then they headed for the chow line.

In the mess hall the distrusting stares of the soldiers were gone. The men had heard about the job Doc, Cyrano and the girls had done in the aid station. Many of the men came over to their table with personal thanks for friends who had been saved. It turned out that most of the men left in that aid station had survived. Medevac choppers came in right after the Cav retook the fire base and had all the wounded out in less than an hour. Those who did die, died from loss of blood due to the fact that all of the supplies of plasma and blood expander had run out.

After dinner Hoang told everyone of his plans to marry Tray. The Monkey Man had hired him as a full time soldier. Hoang was going to work with him as a scout out of their base at the Ranch. The Monkey Man had given Hoang a three day leave after hearing of his marriage plans.

Doc's suspicions about Hoang had pretty much been confirmed by now. He thought back to his last days with the Cav and the night three VC had hit their platoon with RPGs. The Cav had killed two of them right off but somehow one of them had managed to escape. They were just outside of Mai Loc at the time. Hoang had recently admitted that Mai Loc was his home and that's where Doc had first seen Tray. When the Cav came into the Vil the next morning Tray was taken into custody as a suspected sympathizer. Of course Doc had no way of proving it but he was pretty sure Hoang was the one VC who escaped that night.

Since Hoang had saved Docs life on the Plain of Jars he had no desire to press the matter or even to ask Hoang about it. Shit, The Monkey Man must have known it all along. He didn't even seem surprised when Hoang mentioned that Long Tieng was a CIA base. And then the look in Hoang's eyes when The Monkey Man said "only an NVA or VC soldier would know about that."

In a way we're all fighting on the same side Doc thought. The whole idea is just to keep yourself and your friends alive through the insanity.

Chapter 14
Short Timers

The Cav was already saddling up by the time Doc, Cyrano, Hoang and the girls left the mess hall. They got the jeep and pulled into line in front of track three three, Doc's old track.

"Hey lookie there" KC yelled out to Fred "two REMF medics back out in the field."

"Hey Doc" yelled Fred "I thought you were on R and R."

"I am" yelled Doc. "Just got a little lost I think, must have made a wrong turn at the Yellow Brick Road. I'll tell you one thing though, from now on I'm stayin' back in the rear with the beer. I'm too short for this bullshit."

"Thirteen days and a wake up" yelled KC. "I'm one gone mutha fucka."

"Forward hooo" yelled Captain Black and the tracks slowly moved out down the mountain road on their way back to Dong Ha.

Hoang and Tray jumped out of the crowded jeep at the first foot path they came to leading up into the mountains saying it was a shortcut back to their Vil. They invited everyone to their wedding and hoped to see them all soon. Within a few seconds they had disappeared behind a low rocky ravine waving good-bye as they vanished.

"Shortcut my ass" said Cyrano, "they're no where near Mai Loc. Hoang must be lookin' for a little pre-honeymoon action before he has to face up to the mother-in-law." The two girls in the back seat seemed to understand and started giggling again.

But Doc was worried. Something didn't seem right. Hoang looked scared when he left the jeep, almost as though he thought someone would shoot at them the way they disappeared so quickly. He hoped Cyrano was right.

"Hey Cyrano" Doc yelled above the roar of the tracks "what are ya gonna say to Mama San when we show up without one of her girls?"

"Good question" said Cyrano "but I don't think it'll be a problem. I can pay her for Tray with some of the smack. She'll understand it's just one of the risks of her business. I mean it happens to most of her girls eventually, right?"

"Yea, I guess so" said Doc "but I think it'll take more than just a little bit of that stuff to pay for Tray."

"Yea, maybe so but I've got plenty of it."

As the Cav moved down the mountain road the men seemed to be more relaxed than usual, they'd been through a lot of shit in the past few days and they were glad to be on their way back to Dong Ha to finish their stand down time. The thought of another ambush was the furthest thing from their minds.

Chapter 15
Damage Done

On a mountain path high above the Cav, and out of sight from them, Hoang was running now as fast as he could. Tray herself was a good runner but she was having trouble keeping up. She didn't really know what was going on but she new it wasn't good. She yelled at Hoang to slow down but Hoang didn't even look back.

Hoang was breathing hard running up hill. He was concentrating so hard on reaching his friends in time that he did not even feel the pain of oxygen depletion that would have made most men slow down. He rounded a bend in the path still running at top speed and there they were. Their RPG was aimed down hill at the Cav. Hoang yelled out with all his strength using up all the energy he had left. The hand aiming the RPG jerked but the damage had been done and the rocket launched itself down the mountain side. "Whhaaisshh boom" a scream of pain and a desperate cry of "medic" followed by the deafening roar of the Cav's fifty and sixty caliber machine guns all trained on a wisp of smoke fading in a gentle afternoon breeze. The damage had been done!

The Captain was already on the radio to the Dong Ha TOC speaking in the military phonetic code, radio-ese. What he said deciphered was "I need some fast movers and a medevac ASAP. I've got a got target for ya."

"Roger that" said Dong Ha TOC. "But Hit 'em with the Rock Piles one five fives first until the fast movers can get to your position."

"My FO's (Forward Observer, pronounced Foe, man who calls in artillery from distant fire bases.) already on it" said Captain Black.

"You better clear the area right away, there's bound to be some rock slides comin' down the side of that mountain."

"We're on our way, Alpha Six out." The Captain then called to the damaged track. "How bad is it?"

"We've got one man KIA, two seriously wounded, plus three more that need to be medevac'ed."

"How's your track?" Asked the Captain.

"It's still drivable" answered back the driver of the track, the only man on the track not injured.

"OK," said the Captain, "we're going to have to move out to an LZ about three klicks (kilometers) down the hill. Can you make it?"

"Yes sir" answered back the driver.

An M-79 smoke round was fired into the area where the RPG had come from and the tracks quickly moved out down the mountain as the Rock Piles artillery started pounding the area. They hadn't got far when they heard the roar of Phantom jets scream through the sky above them. The jets found their target and dropped several five hundred pound bombs on it throwing rock and debris down the side of the cliff and onto the road below. Although the Cav thought they were a safe distance away they still received a shower of small rocks which bounced off the top of their tracks and the steel pots on their heads.

Doc and Cyrano had been directly in front of the track that had been hit. It was KC's track, one of Docs best friends from his old platoon. He had been sitting in the cupola when the RPG hit it. KC received massive chest injuries but Doc managed to get to him before he died.

Doc knew right away KC didn't stand a chance, he couldn't believe he was still alive. Their was blood everywhere and all the color had left KC's face. His skin had turned to the translucent color of death. There was blood coming out of his mouth. He was breathing fast but didn't seem to be getting any oxygen. Doc could hear the air gurgling through all the holes in his chest. He worked fast, in a few minutes he managed to plug up all the holes with the plastic wrappers from the pressure bandages. The gurgling stopped and KC tried to speak, he spit blood with his words. "Thirteen days man, I'm gonna wake up!" His pupils dilated and seemed to defocus, they turned translucent and his breathing stopped, he was completely still. Doc closed KC's eyes and cried.

The track started moving with the rest of the column, the movement brought Doc back to reality, he started working on the other men but his tears did not stop.

The medevac came in and the dead and wounded were loaded aboard without incident. The fast movers had done a job on the mountain top. The whole area was on fire now, the last two jets had dropped napalm. They left and were replaced by cobra gun ships which flew down low to the ground hovering around looking for anything suspicious to fire at. Occasionally they would open up with rockets or their deadly mini-guns.

Doc figured if that was where Hoang and Tray had been headed their chances for survival were very slim.

After the medevac left Doc got back in the jeep with Cyrano and the girls. The Cav moved out again down the mountain. Doc had regained his composure somewhat, and now had a blank, unemotional stare on his face. He stared straight ahead without saying a word for quite some time. The gunships followed the Cav overhead occasionally opening up on the mountain tops above them.

"Thirteen days man," said Cyrano "I can't believe this shit. It just ain't right. I mean what the fuck are we dyin' for here. The way I see it we've got two choices, either we leave this place or we take it right to the enemy and destroy him."

"Right on," said Doc, "we know where the NVA are hiding. They're on the trail where we're not supposed to go. They're hidin' away in those mountains laughin' at us. I can't take this shit any more. Laos and Cambodia that's where we've got to fight them."

"Yea," said Cyrano, "we could saddle up the whole Cav and take it right down Highway Nine and into Laos."

"The Yellow Brick Road" said Doc.

"Yea man, The Yellow Brick Road, Highway Nine into Laos. It's the only way we're ever gonna be able to win this fucker man. It's gotta be done."

The Cav kept moving down the steep mountain road on its way back to Dong Ha. The next turn on their way was Highway Nine, the Yellow Brick Road.

The Yellow Brick Road had been named by the Cav when they first came into the area. Some called it ambush alley because it was the most likely spot in northern I Corps to be ambushed. The VC and NVA kept the road well guarded because it led straight into Laos and the Ho Chi Min Trail. The road was well named because when you were on the Yellow Brick Road you knew you weren't in Kansas anymore.

KC, who was from Kansas, always found the name quite amusing. He didn't die there but none the less it was one of the last roads he traveled before making the wrong turn to the Rock Pile where the freedom bird (GI slang for the airplane that took them back to the world) took his body home to his family.

Doc thought of this as the Cav continued on down the mountain road headed for Highway Nine and he thought of all the bowls they had shared over the last six months while they rode together on track three three.

The Cav hit the bottom of the mountain on the road leading from the Rock Pile and kept heading south toward Highway Nine. Just before they got to the intersection Doc, Cyrano and most of the rest of the men became very apprehensive. They all knew they were supposed to turn left to Dong Ha but then again this was the Army and nothing was for certain. You never knew when Higher Higher would radio in from TOC and tell the Captain to turn right down the Yellow Brick Road.

Their was a collective sign of relief as the first Sheridan in the column reached the intersection and turned left. The smell of burning marijuana began to fill the air as the men started to unwind from the experiences of the last few days. Doc rolled one up too and passed it to Cyrano.

"Hey Cyrano," said Doc, "just drop me off at Dong Ha. I have no desire to go to Quang Tri, as a matter of fact all I want to do now is sleep."

"You sorry mother!" Said Cyrano. "You mean to say you came all this way and now you want to quit before the mission is finished?"

"That's right" said Doc, "this mission and this war are both nothing but bullshit, I want outa' this place."

"Come on Doc you know better than that. Ain't no way they're gonna let you leave this place 'till your time's up. Don't worry about it man you've got less than five months left to go. Hey, you're a REMF now. You can skate your way home from here."

"Yea I guess you're right but what about KC and all the others, somethin' just ain't right here."

"Yea, I know what ya mean. I know KC was a good friend of yours. I've lost friends that way too, but you gotta keep on keepin' on man, That's what KC was doin' and that's what he'd want you to do now."

"Yea maybe you're right" said Doc. "Hey, we're still on R and R, jeese I forgot all about that. We won't have time to get outa' country but we could hop a C-130 from Quang Tri to China Beach. What da ya say Cyrano?"

"Right on Doc, we owe it to ourselves!"

"Parteee time!" Said Doc as they shook hands in a black brother dap hand shake.

Doc and Cyrano were smiling as the Cav moved on down Highway Nine headed for Dong Ha. They were both thinking about Donut Dollies and cold beer at China Beach when the Cav Troop came to an unexpected stop. The red dust which had been bellowing up behind them caught up with them and blew back over them leaving another layer of the fine red dust on everything, skin, hair, teeth, track, weapons. They even breathed it in through dust coated nostrils into dust coated lungs and then coughed it up and spit it out through dust coated lips.

"Oh shit!" Said Cyrano.

"Now what?" Said Doc with a quiver in his voice which spread through his body. They heard radios breaking squelch up and down the long line of tracks. Then every other track turned in opposite directions facing away from the road. Doc yelled out to the men on the track in front of him, "What the fuck is going on?"

"The Captain just called for a Track Commanders meeting. It looks like Higher Higher doesn't want us back in Dong Ha just yet."

The TC from each track plus Doc and Cyrano gathered in a semi-circle around Captain Blacks track. He leaned against a water can fastened to the back of his track as he stood in the shade, waiting for the men to settle down. The squawk of his many radios could be heard in the background as he started to speak. "Men, I'm afraid I've got some bad news. We won't be returning to Dong Ha for a few more days. TOC just sent us an order from Higher Higher." Captain Black paused for a second to see the reaction from his troops.

A low murmuring groan came from them punctuated by a few cries of "Sheeeit!"

The Captain continued. "Apparently the same regiment of NVA that we chased away from the Rock Pile is using the hills around Khe Sanh for a staging and resupply area. The Khe Sanh area belongs to Charley, it always has and maybe it always will. You all know the story of the Marines hanging on to Khe Sanh. The place is right next to the Laotian border and the Ho Chi Minh Trail so they can be resupplied easily. If they run into a lot of us they can always run across the border where we're not allowed to follow."

The men all laughed at this, most of them had been across that border before or at least they thought they had. Captain Black laughed along with them, having led most of these men into Laos just a few months ago.

"At any rate our orders are to find the enemy's hiding places and to chase him back across the border to the trail where our B-52s will take care of them. I know it doesn't sound like a job that can be done in a few days but our FAC pilots have been searching the area and say they have their positions pinpointed. Air strikes have already been called on them, but they're dug in too deep for the Air Force. Are there any questions?"

"Yea," said Doc, "we've got two civilians with us that we've got to get back to Quang Tri, and me and Cyrano here are supposed to be on R and R."

Laughter broke out again from the troops.

"I'd like to let you guys go" said Captain Black "but I'm afraid the road is too dangerous to let you go back by yourselves."

"We're willing to take our chances." Said Cyrano. "We made it out here all alone without any problems and I'm sure we can make it back. From here to Quang Tri the roads are pretty damn secure."

"That's all very well and good Cyrano but you're with me now and when you're with me you're my responsibility. You know I can't take those kind of chances. If something were to happen to you it would be my fault for letting you go. Besides we're short on medics here and we could use both you guys and the two women. I heard about the outstanding job they did in the Rock Pile aid station. Since they're civilians though I'm afraid we'll have to send them back tonight with the resupply chopper."

A loud groan came from the men. Most of them knew Cyrano, and even the ones who didn't knew what the girls were doing with him.

"Now I want you to hook that jeep up to track three three with a tow bar. That thing's too dangerous to drive out here, what with the mines and all. Two of the guns have been damaged on the track so we'll take out most of the ammunition and resupply it with medical equipment."

"Just a few more days men and we'll all be in the rear for some R and R. Now let's mount up and get this over with."

The men slowly made their way back to their tracks, muffling curses under their breath. Some were not well muffled. When they got back to their tracks and told the rest of the men the new orders there were more curses. Joints were lit and passed between the men. Most of the men were used to this sort of thing by now and the new guys who weren't soon would be. They were all afflicted by the same malady. The curse of the men who had to do the fighting never being able to make the decisions.

Chapter 16
Three Escape The Cav

The radios broke squelch and the familiar cry was heard "Forward *haoow*!" Highway Nine, the Yellow Brick Road, hadn't been used much in recent times by any of the Americans. It was pretty much Charlie's country. The last time the road had been used by anything but the Cav's tracks was when the Marines defended the place during the siege of Khe Sanh which reached its climax during the Tet offensive early in 1968. The Yellow Brick Road had not been repaired since that time. The VC had managed to blow up all the bridges and no doubt they had planted a liberal number of mines and booby traps all along the road.

By noon it had become very hot, the temperature had passed 110 degrees without so much as a breeze and the going was slow. The column was now being led by a mine sweeping tank, and every half hour or so they had to stop the column and wait for the demolition crew to blow a mine. It was miserable on top of the tracks with the unrelenting sun beating down on the men in their heavy flack jackets and steel pots.

"I can't even believe I'm still doin' this shit" said Doc as he wiped his sweat and dust caked face off with an olive drab towel that was dirtier than his face.

"Fire in the hole!" One of the demolition crew members yelled out as he triggered a remote controlled explosion to set off a mine in the road. The explosion was far bigger than anyone was expecting. They all ducked for cover as dirt, rocks, and shrapnel rained down on them. Their was a blood curdling scream from the front of the column and then the cry of "Medic!"

Cyrano, who was sitting in the cupola as the acting track commander, hit the drivers Fiberglas communications helmet with a bamboo walking stick and then remembering the intercom mike on his helmet he yelled "Go!" to the driver. The diesel engine of the track roared as it sped off around the tracks in front of them.

By the time they got to the mine sweep tank the crew had already lifted the injured man to the ground. He was laying there squirting blood from a hole in his shoulder where a large piece of shrapnel had lodged itself.

The man was screaming because the metal was red hot. Steam and the smell of burning flesh were coming from the wound along with the squirting blood. Doc unclasped one of the haemostatic clamps which always hung from his shirt pocket and yelled "Make sure somebody's called a medevac." Then he probed around the wound with the tip of the clamp looking for the source of the blood which continued to squirt in alarming profusion. It seemed like there was blood everywhere. Doc found the torn artery and clamped it off, finally stopping the flow of blood.

The man had stopped screaming but he was pale and losing consciousness. Doc figured he must be going into shock. He yelled at Cyrano to bring down some plasma from the track.

They moved the wounded man out of the hot sun and placed him on a stretcher in the shade of the mine sweep tank.

Cyrano came down from the medic track with the plastic bag of plasma. He had a hard time finding a vein in the man's arm but after a few minutes of probing he managed to insert the needle. He hung the bag of plasma from the treads of the tank and then said to Doc "Looks like the girls 'ill be skyin' now."

"Yea," said Doc "wish I was goin' with 'em. I feel like I've been drafted all over again. Some R and R huh?"

"Hey be cool Doc." said Cyrano, "We'll make it out of here all right, no sweat."

"Hey Cyrano" said Doc as he tried to wipe his face dry one more time with the dirty towel "I'm sweatin'! And speakin' of sweatin' what are you going to do about Tray and Mama San."

"Yea, that's right" said Cyrano. "I guess I better take care of that right now before the chopper gets here."

"Yea, I guess you better" said Doc as he went back to work checking the vital signs of the wounded man.

Cyrano climbed down through the open hatch of the medic track. The girls were sitting inside the track huddled together. They looked tired and scared. The men had told them several times to get up on top where they would be safer from land mines and RPGs but they pretended not to understand and refused to move. They didn't care much for the Cav or what they'd been through the past few days. They wanted to go back home to Quang Tri. Life there may not have been easy but anything would be better than this.

"You go home now" Cyrano said to them. The girls gave him a slightly tearful smile. "I don't know if Tray is still alive or not but at any rate she won't be returning to Mama Sans with you so I'll have to pay Mama San for her." Cyrano dug through his wet bag and pulled out what he figured was about a pound of heroin and gave it to the girls. "Now make sure no one sees this until you give it to Mama San in Quang Tri, OK?" The girls both nodded their heads and one of them put the little bundle of heroin into her bamboo bag and covered it up with some spare clothing.

Through the open hatch of the track above them came the whackety whack whack of the Medical Evacuation helicopter as it came in from a distance. As it grew louder all three of them looked up to the sky in anticipation. "Come on" said Cyrano, "lets go." The girls hesitated for a second and then they both hugged him with sobs and tears, though they were smiling. They were smiling because they knew they were going home.

Cyrano and the girls climbed through the hatch of the track just as the chopper appeared overhead. They climbed down to the ground and stood next to Doc and the wounded soldier as one of the men threw a can of green smoke to mark the landing zone for the medevac. The smoke canister ignited with the sound of a firecracker and the bright green smoke billowed out in swirls as the chopper began to descend.

They all braced themselves against the wind from the descending bird as it threw sand, small pebbles and the swirling green smoke at them. When it touched down Cyrano and another man picked up the stretcher and began running toward the chopper while Doc held the plasma bag above the injured man. The girls followed them shielding their eyes from the flying debris. They handed off the stretcher to the helicopter crew and then the girls jumped in. One of them grabbed Docs hand as the chopper's engine began to rev. They looked at each other as the chopper started to lift off and saw the sorrow in each others eyes. As the bird pulled their hands apart they realized how much life and death they had shared in such a short time.

As the chopper took to the sky the girls were awed by the sight before them. The rushing wind from the open chopper doors dried their tears and they smiled as they watched their motherland rush by below them.

Back at Quang Tri the story of the battle for the Rock Pile had been told many times. The courage of the three women had not gone unnoticed. The higher ups, thinking the girls were ARVN (Army of the Republic of Vietnam) nurses, had put them in for bronze stars after consulting with Captain Black by radio.

Some of the wounded men who weren't seriously injured were recovering at the MASH unit in Quang Tri. As is usually the case in these situations, some of the men's stories had been exaggerated over the past few days. In particular the exploits of Fingers, The Monkey Man and what now was being called their A Team. Somehow Military Intelligence had "leaked" information possibly as a morale booster for the soldiers of I Corps. According to the story Fingers and The Monkey Man had joined forces with a Company of Airborne Rangers and had kicked the asses of a large number of unfriendlies in their Laotian sanctuary on the Plain of Jars. Word had it that the Rangers were so hyped up on revenge over what happened at the Rock Pile they didn't even bother to use their weapons. They snuck up on the enemy at night and wiped out the entire unit with nothing but fists and knives.

Chapter 17
The Yellow Brick Road

When the medevac chopper arrived in Quang Tri it was met by a military band playing the Star Spangled Banner. After the injured soldier was removed there was an awards ceremony. The two girls were given their Bronze Stars. One was also awarded to Tray although she was now considered missing in action.

After the ceremony the girls were offered jobs with the Mash unit at Quang Tri combat base. Since the pay was far better than what they were making as prostitutes they both accepted. They were given a ride back to Mama San's place in a Colonels jeep with a military escort of MPs. Mama San thought she was being busted and hid in her bomb shelter beneath the hootch until the MPs left. She was understandably surprised when the girls gave her a pound of pure uncut China White heroin compliments of Cyrano. It helped to ease her sorrow over the loss of Tray.

Back on the Yellow Brick Road the Cav was having a tough time of it. Their orders were to make it to the old Khe Sanh combat base before dark. Hopefully with enough time to dig in before the sun set behind the mountains of Laos. The day was moving on and at the rate they were going they'd never make it. Not only was the road well planted with mines but all of the bridges had long since been blown by the NVA. The going was far too slow and Captain Black knew he had to do something about it. He realized it might mean sacrificing some of his men and their machines but it had to be done. Better to sacrifice a few than to lose the whole Troop. Khe Sanh was on a large and flat mountain top. It had good fields of fire from every direction. It was the safest place around to set up and they had to make it there before dark.

Captain Black got on the radio and told his men they would have to give up on the mine sweep. He asked for a volunteer, one man to drive a track, the Sheridans were too valuable to risk. The volunteer had to have sharp eyes to detect any irregularities in the dirt road's surface. The man's orders were to "Drive as far off to one side of the trail as possible, keep your eyes open and keep going at full throttle no matter what." As an after thought Captain Black added, "A little praying might not hurt either."

Five men volunteered, a deck of cards was placed before them and they drew from the deck. High card would be the first driver the other men would follow in descending order if necessary. "If we lose any more than five tracks we probably won't make it anyway" said Captain Black.

Two tracks were emptied of men and anything else of value to the mission. They were brought to the front of the column each with only one driver.

Captain Black had agonized over this decision for some time knowing that the volunteers would most likely hit a mine and if it was one of the big ones say a five hundred pounder it would mean certain death for the driver. He had seen it happen before. That's why he waited 'til it was the last possible option, until he knew there would not be enough time to make it to Khe Sanh at the slow pace they were traveling. The dilemma was as old as war itself. The few had to be sacrificed for the survival of the whole. He knew it was the right decision but still it bothered him to have to make it. At times like this he still wondered if, even after all this time, he truly was cut out to be a leader of men. Although he didn't realize it at the time, it was this very quality which made him a great leader. Despite their occasional grumbles the men liked Captain Black. They new he was willing to take any risk he expected the men to take and they knew he cared.

Captain Black got on the radio and called out to his men "Forward haoww." The tracks roared and even after all they'd been through, and all they knew they were yet to face, the men answered the call once more "yee haaa!"

Within a few seconds the long column of tracks was roaring down the Yellow Brick Road at top speed, the tracks bouncing over the rough dirt road. The lead track with only a driver struck a course just to the right of the trail-like road as fast as the track would go keeping his eyes peeled on the ground before him. His reflexes were keen. He quickly steered the track to avoid even the slightest irregularity in the road. The drivers behind him did not have things any easier. They had to follow exactly in his tracks without even the slightest deviation. Any one of the tracks that failed to do this stood a good chance of hitting a mine.

They made good time, and although all the bridges were out, the rivers were low and the Cav had no trouble fording them. The terrain was becoming mountainous and the road less well worn. The driver of the first track had seen and avoided many spots in the road which he was sure were freshly planted mines. What he worried most about though were the old ones. Erosion from the rains could have easily made them invisible to his keen eyes.

The Cav was getting close to their objective. The mountains of Laos were now visible ahead of them. If they could keep up the pace for another hour they would make it to Khe Sanh with enough time to dig in before nightfall.

The hills were closing in on the road though. Even the jungle seemed to be moving in closer. This was ambush country. The men could feel the stare of eyes upon their backs, but when they turned to look there was nothing but jungle.

They were scared, no one was nodding off at his gun no matter how tired he might be. They could feel the tension in the air. Their weapons were at the ready, the men's muscles cocked and on a hair trigger. Despite their high rate of speed every motion the jungle made was quickly met by a host of eyeballs and gun barrels. Every bird, every monkey, every wild bore, every breeze strong enough to move a blade of grass. The men were scared but they knew their strength was in their fire power. They did not want to die and they put their faith in the awesome fire power of the Cav.

"Kaaa whaaamm" the shock wave from the explosion hit the men first then the chunks of hot metal, the shrapnel and the chunks of dirt and stone. The pieces of the unfortunate Armored Personnel carrier along with more dirt and rock rained down on them for what seemed like an eternity.

Instinctively the tracks turned into their defensive herringbone pattern and began opening up on the tree line with their machine guns. As they did so two more tracks hit mines in the road. They were smaller ones but still packed enough force to put the tracks out of commission. RPGs and light arms fire began coming in on the Cav from the tree line as the NVA sprung their ambush. The men of the Cav fired back with renewed force now that they had a fix on their enemies position. The Sheridan tanks opened up with their big guns on spots in the tree line with the heaviest concentration of enemy fire. Tracks were being hit with RPG fire and several of them burst into flames their ammunition cooking off into more explosions in the hot fires.

The men looked around waiting for orders but none came. "Holy shit" said Cyrano to Doc. "The track that hit the first mine was in the center of the column, it must have been Captain Black's track."

"Yea" said Doc "it had to have been a command detonated mine."

"No doubt," said Cyrano, "I just wish someone would take over his command before we get blown to shit here."

Finally one of the platoon lieutenants came over the radio. "Hold your positions men and conserve your ammunition, don't fire unless you've got a target. I've got air and art'y on the way."

A few seconds later a marker round exploded over the tree line before them followed by a barrage of one five five round explosions in the same spot. "That oughta take care of them" said Doc. A few seconds more and Cobra gun ships arrived and started hosing down the same tree line with their mini-guns.

Except for an occasional sniper the enemy fire stopped. Master Sergeant Macintosh came on the horn. "Medics get to work you've got dead and wounded to be taken care of. I want everybody policed up and on the tracks in five mikes 'cause that's when we're movin' aut ah here." Then the Sergeant called into Dong Ha TOC and asked for some fast movers to drop napalm on the tree-line. They answered back that they were already on the way and would be there in five minutes. "Perfect timing" said the top Sergeant.

Sergeant Macintosh was the top ranking NCO and the oldest man in the Cav Troop. He had survived the Korean War and planned to survive this one too. That's why he had a tendency to take charge in situations like this one. Since Captain Black was dead he was outranked by each of the Troop's three platoon leaders, who were young Lieutenants. The Lieutenants were afraid of him though, and never messed with him. Sergeant Macintosh was admired by everyone, enlisted men and officers alike. They all called him 'Top'. The title seemed to fit.

The Cav Troop had one medic to each platoon plus a medic track filled with medical supplies along with two medics. Unfortunately for Doc and Cyrano it had hit a large mine over a month ago and still hadn't been replaced. That's why Captain Black had pounced on the opportunity to keep Doc and Cyrano with the Troop. They had both served with him in the field in the past. Unfortunately for Captain Black though there was nothing they could do for him this time. Captain Black's number was up and there wasn't enough of him left to fill up a body bag.

Within five minutes the medics had managed to bandage up the wounded and load the dead back onto the tracks. The last thing they did was to find what was left of Captain Black and the other men from his command track.

When Sergeant Mac ordered the column to move out the jets were already screaming in on their approach to the enemy positions in the tree line. The lead F-14 dropped its load of napalm just as the Cav Troop cleared the area. The men on top the tracks were close enough to feel the heat from the burning napalm and to feel the wind sucked by them that fed the inferno.

Sergeant Mac figured they still had time to make it to Khe Sanh before nightfall but he didn't like the losses they had suffered in such a short time. They had been lucky at the Rock Pile only losing one Sheridan tank. The Yellow Brick Road was proving to be another story. Since they were ordered to turn around they had lost two armored personal carriers to mines, one of them Captain Blacks track to a command detonated mine which started the ambush. The ambush itself proved to be the most damaging incident so far, they lost another two tracks right away when they rolled onto mines on the road getting into a defensive position. The worst part though was the three tracks they lost to RPGs during the ambush.

Sergeant Mac was worried. He knew there was a lot of shit just waiting to come down on them at Khe Sanh if they were lucky enough to make it that far. "Luck" Sergeant Mac thought to himself.

He hated being in a position where he had to depend on luck for the survival of his men.

The caravan of tracks and Sheridan tanks was moving out at top speed headed for Khe Sanh down a rough dirt road that looked more like a trail than a road. While the men of the Cav all called it the yellow Brick Road, it was called Highway Nine on the maps.

Doc and Cyrano had been nodding off from lack of sleep. Their track hit a large bump which woke up Cyrano with a start. For a second he thought they'd hit a mine. He looked to his left side and saw Doc leaning against the cupola with his eyes closed and yelled in his ear. "Hey Doc wake up, we're off to see the Wizard."

"Ah shit" said Doc. "First off to see the Jars and now off to see the Wizard, you're nuts man, I should have never listened to ya. I could have been on R and R right now."

"Well Doc," said Cyrano, "you said you wanted to find out what this war was about."

"Yea" said Doc, "and so far it looks like it's about heroin and opium."

"Maybe so" said Cyrano.

"And speaking of wizards," said Doc, "what do you think of that tribe member, that Shaman who gave me this pouch filled with liquid opium?"

"That was some really strange shit," said Cyrano, "I don't know what to make of it but it sure as hell impressed Hoang. Remember how he bowed down to him like the guy was some sort of a god? That tribe was truly strange. They seemed to be in complete control of everything that was going on. And then the way they escaped from us. I mean the whole tribe, elephants and all just disappeared into thin air. I wanted to ask Hoang about it but I never got a chance to."

"Yea," said Doc, "it doesn't look like we'll ever see Hoang or Tray again. They were headed right for that ambush site at the Rock Pile and I don't think anyone could have survived that."

"No shit," said Cyrano, "it looks like they were VC after all."

"Good people though for VC" said Doc. "I mean the guy did save my life at the battle of the Plain of Jars."

"Yea," said Cyrano, "that was some battle. I swear that tribe stopped the guns from working. And what about that rocket or whatever it was that took off just before we got to the crashed planes?"

"Yea" said Doc "and T Rex."

"Shit" said Cyrano, "this is all just too much to believe, maybe… maybe we just imagined the whole thing."

"Yea," said Doc, "it must be battle fatigue."

"Maybe that's it!" Said Cyrano. "I tell ya I sure as hell feel like I've got battle fatigue!"

"Yea," said Doc "me too!"

The Cav Troop moved on at top speed like a caravan of Gypsies on their way to a rendezvous with the devil.

Kaa-boom, flying dust and debris, the lead track jumped several feet into the air came down with a broken tread, slid several yards then rolled onto its side and slid another twenty yards before it ground to a stop alongside the Yellow Brick Road. "Don't stop," yelled Sergeant Mac to the column of tracks through his radio, "Drive on!"

The driver of the wrecked track miraculously climbed out through the drivers hatch. Doc and Cyrano's medic track pulling their jeep behind it broke from the column and pulled up to the dazed driver. "Hop on" yelled Cyrano. The man shakily grabbed the hand hold at the rear of their track and slowly began pulling himself up. Doc grabbed his other arm and quickly pulled him up top just as a burst of AK fire erupted from the tree line. The rounds crashed into the side of their track with a dull metallic clank.

"Let's get the fuck outta here!" Said Doc. The medic track raced back into the column and the Cav Troop continued on without slowing down.

The driver of the blown up track gave Doc a confused look and asked "Where am I?"

"Ya don't wanna know!" Said Doc.

Several of the tracks took small arms fire from the tree line and opened up with their machine guns. They were lucky once again and suffered no serious injuries. After less than a minute of firing Sergeant Mac ordered the troops to cease fire, he was worried about running low on ammunition.

One of the lieutenants called in an air strike on the sight of the ambush. The men could hear the explosions from behind them as they caught their first sight of the abandoned Khe Sanh Combat Base. Since it had been completely abandoned two years ago, in 1968, there wasn't much to see. Few of the men realized the large flat topped hill before them was the now legendary Khe Sanh. There was nothing left there from when the Marines had occupied the place. The entire area had been bulldozed to prevent the NVA from using the bunkers.

As they began making the climb to the hill top, and the men realized where they were, the level of fear rose another notch. "So this is the infamous Khe Sanh" said Doc.

"Yea, I guess so" said Cyrano, "it sure looks deserted,"

"It may look that way" said Doc, "but I feel like I'm being watched by a thousand eyes."

"I hate that feeling" said Cyrano.

As they reached the top of the hill Sergeant Mac told the men to set up in the middle of the hill next to the old landing strip. The metal landing surface had been removed but, except for a few shell holes and a little soil erosion from the monsoon rains, the landing strip looked like it could still be used. It would be a bumpy landing but it could be done.

The tracks and Sheridan tanks pulled into their covered wagon style circle next to the runway and Sergeant Mac gave the order "Dig in troops, dig in fast and deep it's going to be a long night!"

Chapter 18
Americanization

Hoang and Tray had escaped the American bombing in one of the many deep rock caves. The mountains were filled with such caves and the VC took full advantage of them. One of the most famous of these was the huge cave inside of Marble Mountain at Da Nang. The VC used it as a hospital even though it was right next to a large American base. The GIs never even knew it was there.

At the village of Mai Loc preparations for tomorrow's ceremony were already well under way. The elders of the village were disappointed in the fact that the old traditions were not being followed anymore. It was because of the war, the war was destroying their way of life, the spirits of their ancestors who still inhabited the land could become angry causing poor crops and starvation for the future. But with the war going on there was just no time for the old ways. The elders hoped and prayed that the spirits of their ancestors would understand.

It didn't seem to matter whether they fought with the Americans or against them. Either way they became more like the Americans.

Hoang had returned to the village with great wealth. He was now by far the richest man in his village. The wedding ceremony would share some of this wealth with the rest of the village.

Chapter 19
Bad Troop's Pay

In the Secret City of Long Tieng an argument was raging between an Air Force Colonel and a CIA Case Officer. "Sir," said the Case Officer, "you just don't understand. If we want to continue fighting this war we have to let the Hmong sell their opium, it's their only source of money. Since we're officially not even here, how do you expect the pentagon to fund us. They're having problems accounting for what they give us already. I don't like it any better than you sir but without the opium money we're out of here and the war will be lost. I don't just mean in Laos, I mean Vietnam too."

"God damn it" said the Air Force Colonel, "how did we ever get into this position, I can't believe I'm doing this. Don't you realize what's going on. They're making heroin out of the opium right here in Long Tieng. We're transporting it for them in our planes and do you know where that heroin is going? It's going right to our own fighting men in Vietnam. We're making addicts out of our own kids for Christ sake. I just can't do this."

"You don't have any choice in the matter and you know it sir. Our soldiers in Vietnam will survive it, at least the good ones will. In a month you'll be state side and you can forget about the whole thing. I'm just sorry you had to find out!"

The Air Force Colonel stomped off to the officers club muttering under his breath. He stared straight ahead ignoring the salute of a young mechanic as he passed by him. He sat down at the bar and proceeded to get drunk.

Chapter 20
Creative Funding

Back at the Ranch the Special Forces Captain was in a meeting with a hand picked team of Green Berets. The Monkey Man was their leader and Fingers was second in command.

"I don't need to tell you men just how important this mission is. As you well know the United States has already begun pulling troops out of Vietnam. Because of that we are going to have to win this war in a hurry. If we can't do it in the next year it isn't going to happen at all. Not only is the United States pulling out its men, it's also cutting its funding for the war.

The purpose of this mission is to secure funding for both the Saigon government and the Hmong Army in Laos. Your job will be to act as a security force making sure that all the elements involved in this operation work together. Those elements are the Hmong Army lead by General Vang Pao, the US Air Force, the CIA, the

Army of the Republic of Vietnam and a troop of the US Army's Armored Cavalry. These elements do not always work well together so stay alert for any problems. The Cavalry Troop is already at the Khe Sanh landing strip securing the area. The Air Force will be landing a C-130 at Khe Sanh, with them will be several CIA case officers and General Vang Pao with several of his soldiers. The Saigon government will be landing another C-130 carrying several ARVN soldiers. As you well know the ARVNs and the Hmong do not trust each other. Gentlemen it will not be easy keeping these elements working together.

Chapter 21
Khe Sanh

At the outpost of Khe Sanh the sun had set behind the mountains of Laos and the darkness was creeping in. The resupply helicopters were landing on the old air strip with their badly needed loads of ammunition. They landed without incident and their crews quickly began kicking the crates of ammo out the open doors as the dead and wounded were loaded aboard a medevac helicopter. They had been escorted in by several Cobra attack choppers who circled the hill top looking for anything suspicious.

Several explosions were heard, and felt, a few hundred yards from the unloading helicopters. The cry of "Incoming" was yelled out and the men worked even faster, *running* the ammo crates back into the Cav's perimeter. The explosions kept coming closer. "Mortars!" one of the men yelled out. "They're walkin' em in."

One helicopter lifted off just in time as several rounds dropped right on the spot it had occupied. The men from the Cav were forced back into their perimeter where they sought the shelter of their holes. "Let's get a fix on the sound from those tubes." Sergeant Mac yelled into the radio. "If the Cobras can't get 'em we'll give the Sheridans a chance to show us what they can do with their bag guns."

The Cobras found the mortar tubes and opened up on them with their mini-guns and rockets. Fire rained down on the positions from the sky, and the mortars stopped. Immediately tracer rounds from a big antiaircraft gun could be seen slamming into one of the Cobras. It started to rise up back into the sky, shuddered for a second as though it had hit a bump in the air, then it exploded and burst into flames, finally falling to the ground in several flaming pieces.

The Cav opened up on the distant hill with its fifty caliber machine guns and the Sheridan main guns. The antiaircraft fire stopped and the remaining Cobra helicopters raced to the area to make sure it wouldn't be starting up again. They expended the rest of their rockets and mini-gun ammunition on the area.

The Cav sent out a quickly organized patrol to recover the bodies from the downed chopper in the fading light. The Cobras hovered above them hoping for survivors as the men pulled the charred bodies from the wreckage. They wrapped the bodies in ponchos as another medevac came in to take them away. The Medevac landed and left in a hurry escorted by the Cobras.

As Doc and Cyrano came back in through the wire with the patrol Cyrano said to Doc, "Well, I guess they know where we are now."

"Yea," said Doc "I guess!"

Squelch broke on the tracks radios and Sergeant Mac's voice crackled out "Double guard duty tonight boys and for the next thirty I want everyone in their holes. The Rock Pile just got some new guns today, one seven five Howitzers. I asked them to use our area to sight them in so we'll have rounds going off all around us. As you men already know we also have a large concentration of NVA all around us so we should thank the Lord for those big guns, or at least thank the American tax payers. Button up boys the fire mission will commence in two minutes."

Exactly two minutes later plus the number of seconds it took for the rounds to travel the distance a screaming roar was heard over the Cav's defensive circle. The men all looked up from their holes, following the sound with their eyes.

As was standard operating procedure, the first rounds were white phosphorus marking rounds just in case someone had the coordinates wrong. White phosphorus although less dangerous than the high explosive rounds could still cause serious injuries to the troops. Instead of throwing out jagged chunks of shrapnel they exploded into thousands of pieces of a burning white goo which stuck to everything it touched. The real problem with the stuff was that it was almost impossible to put out. It even burned under water. It would burn into human flesh until it burned itself up. Doc and Cyrano had been taught to smother it with mud but unless it was the monsoon season mud wasn't easy to find on hilltops. It took time to make it with the Cav's own supply of water. Even when there was plenty of mud the medics had discovered that it didn't work nearly as well as they had been taught it would in training. Doc thought of this as he watched the marker rounds explode on target a safe distance from their perimeter and then heard the FO yell "Fire for effect" into his radio.

The rounds once more screamed over their heads and then crunched into the earth with deafening explosions which shook the ground all around them. They kept coming in, on and on. Doc wished they would stop but he knew they would not. The sound brought back memories. The memories from just a month ago, back when he was still with the Cav. The memories of the human wave attack. The screams of the men were the worst part. First there was the inhuman screams of the charging enemy. So many of them at first that they drowned out the sounds of the machine guns that were cutting them down. Slowly these screams changed to screams of terror, screams of death, then to the screams of his own men as their position was overrun. Finally came the screams of the artillery rounds as they crashed into their own perimeter killing everyone who wasn't in a deep hole, and eventually came a deafening silence on the body strewn battle field.

Cyrano slapped Doc on the back. "Hey man come out of it. You're startin' ta develop the thousand yard stare."

"Shit man," said Doc, "I've gotta get outa this place before I lose my mind."

"Sorry," said Cyrano, "nobody gets outa here without either losing their mind or their life, take your pick, which will it be!"

The artillery barrage turned silent as the full darkness of night slowly crept through the defensive perimeter of the Cav Troop.

The men were on double watch, they were alert, every muscle tensed. Eyes wide open staring straight ahead into the darkness. The good ones had learned how to use the corners of their vision to detect movement in the dark. "If you look right at them in the darkness they will disappear" they would say. "Keep them at the corners of your vision."

Every sound brought dozens of guns to bare on its perceived source. The men not on guard tried to sleep but for most it was a hopeless cause. Doc was so tired he managed to fall asleep. A track started its engine to recharge its batteries and Doc dreamt of the dozers, their plows scraping the ground filled with the dead bodies from the Chinese human wave attack. Shoving them into a mass grave.

The Rock Pile's artillery started up again with harassment fire and Docs eyes sprung open. For a second he thought he heard the screams again but the artillery stopped and there was only silence as he stared up out of his hole at the brilliant stars above him in a dark sky.

"Whisssh boom!" An RPG exploded against the wire RPG screen in front of one of the tracks, and the Cav opened up instantly in all directions with everything it had. "Cease fire, cease fire." yelled Sergeant Mac, "Conserve your ammo" but it took several minutes before the men let off enough tension to quit firing. Sergeant Mac got back on the horn and scolded his men about wasting ammunition, then climbed down from his Sheridan tank and took a walk around the perimeter with the three lieutenants. He gave the men words of encouragement and tried to impress upon them the importance of conserving ammunition. "We know they're out there" he said to one trooper "but as long as we've got ammunition they're not coming in here. When you fire your weapon make sure you have a target." He and the Lieutenants checked the ammunition supplies of each track.

He figured they had been lucky, the choppers had managed to kick out most of their resupply even though they had been under fire. The track floors were filled with ammo cans almost to their capacity. They figured three rows deep covering the track floor was the maximum amount of weight the tracks could take. They had about two and a half rows and Sergeant Mac figured even two rows should be enough as long as the men didn't waste it. The problem was though, the men liked to fire their weapons whenever they could, it made them feel more secure. Sergeant Mac looked at it as a lack of discipline. It was his job to teach them discipline.

The Cav was harassed all night with sniper fire, RPGs and mortars. Sergeant Mac figured he had done a good job keeping their firing down to a minimum. They called in the Rock Pile's artillery often and close. So close that shrapnel was bouncing off the tracks and thudding into their perimeter. It was dangerous all right, one man had a hot piece glance off his helmet and another man had a piece tear a hunk of muscle out of his shoulder. Doc managed to stop the bleeding right away and figured he was in no danger, he could wait 'til morning for a medevac.

Sergeant Mac didn't like calling in the art'y this close. He knew the dangers well and had seen the results many times. Still, it was a question of the lesser of two evils. Without the close artillery the gooks would be in the wire and the men would have to use their valuable ammunition to keep them back.

Sergeant Mac knew that his men didn't have enough fire discipline to conserve their ammo so it would last 'til morning. He also knew if they ran out of ammo they would all be dead. Once again a few would have to be sacrificed for the survival of the Troop. Sergeant Mac didn't like it but that's the way things were.

The darkness of the night moved on ever so slowly. About two o'clock they began receiving sporadic incoming mortar fire. The men were dug in deep so it would take a direct hit in one of their holes to hurt anyone. It kept the men awake but the fact was it didn't pose much of a threat except to the one man on top of each track.

"FO get a fix on the sound from that mortar tube and knock it out before they hit one of our tracks" Sergeant Mac called out over the radio.

"I think I've already got it" said FO as three artillery rounds screamed high over their heads and crashed with a fiery explosion on a nearby hill.

A scream was heard and then once again total silence broken only by a yell from one of the troops "gotchyr sorry ass Charlie." This was followed by another yell but in Vietnamese from off in the distance. The men didn't understand the words but they caught the meaning all right. There were plenty more of them out there. The artillery duel kept up most of the night interspersed with long periods of silence.

About three o'clock the NVA managed to land a lucky round right on top of one of the tracks. It killed the man on guard duty at the fifty instantly. Half an hour later another lucky shot landed in one of the men's holes killing him also. The Cav kept firing back with the Rock Pile's big guns but it was obvious they were up against a large enemy force which had Khe Sanh surrounded.

It was about four AM when the NVA started their attack. Sappers had been moving slowly and quietly through the wire and were almost inside the Cav's perimeter when one of them set off a well set trip flare. The yell was heard above the roar of an already firing fifty caliber machine gun "gooks in the wire!"

The Cav once again opened up with everything they had but this time Sergeant Mac didn't try to stop his troops. He knew this time it was for real. Three of the tracks burst into flames instantly from NVA Rocket Propelled Grenades. There were explosions everywhere from mortars and RPGs.

Some of the men fired off their pop up flares. Sergeant Mac told FO to call for illumination rounds from the Rock Pile. Within minutes the Cav's perimeter was lit up like a night time football field back in the world. Surprisingly though there were few enemy targets in the wire. The few that were visible though drew red tracers from the Cav's machine guns. The bodies of the unfortunate NVA soldiers seemed to dance to an inhumanly fast beat for a few seconds before they exploded. The intense gun fire seemed to suspend the bodies in the air while they were torn to pieces, and the cross fire from several tracks threw blood, chunks of flesh and bone, and whole body parts, in every direction.

Suddenly explosions started coming from what seemed to be the wrong direction. Satchel charges were exploding from behind the tracks inside the Cav's perimeter. The mortar pit must have been hit by two or three of them at the same time. The mortar tube went flying into the air along with several bodies and a large quantity of unexploded mortar rounds. A few of these went off in secondary explosions.

Satchel charges were being dropped into the men's fighting holes from behind. Men went flying into the air screaming their last scream and landing limp and dead on the ground around their holes. Small weapons fire began slamming into the tracks from behind and gradually the men started to figure out they were being hit from both sides. The cry went out from track to track and hole to hole. No one even considered using a radio, things were too hectic and the holes didn't have radios anyway. "Tunnels, they've got tunnels!" The big machine guns couldn't be turned around it was too dangerous, they'd kill their own men. M16s and 45s were picked up. Shotguns and M79s with shotgun loads. They were aimed carefully and many shots hit their marks but it was inevitable that a few friendly fire hits would be taken, it just couldn't be helped in the confusion.

It was later said that two of the young lieutenants died that way but no one would admit to it and there was no way it could be proved. Some of the enemy soldiers used the same small arms as the Cav.

Sergeant Mac got on the horn to the track on either side of him. "Three four and three eight cover my position I'm going into the middle of the rond (the covered wagon style circle the Cav set up in) to plug up some of those tunnels." He turned his Sheridan tank around and roared into the center of the perimeter firing his fifty into the ground at anything that looked suspicious. Small arms fire erupted in his direction clanking off the armor of his tank, then RPGs exploded glancing off his tank and throwing shrapnel in every direction.

He kept moving until he was almost on top of the tunnel which was inside the mortar pit. The enemy soldiers had been using the mortar pit for cover. A few of them fled when they saw him coming and were cut down by the Cav's small arms fire. The rest kept fighting until he was right on them. He started firing his main gun at point blank range right into the hole. As they crashed into the pit he ordered the driver to do pirouettes over the hole. The few enemy soldiers who were still alive managed to clamor back into the tunnel where they were crushed to death by the weight of the spinning tank as it caved in the tunnel. The ones who didn't make it down the hole were quickly turned to hamburger by the treads of the Sheridan as it spun.

Doc, Cyrano and the other medics were kept busy as the battle raged on. The NVA soldiers were storming the perimeter wire with suicidal abandonment. The Cav cut them down with machine gun fire, and the Sheridan tanks main guns, which were now firing fleshet rounds. These were like giant shotgun shells only instead of buckshot they fired thousands of little steel darts.

The enemy kept up the pressure till sunrise when they gave up and slowly broke contact just before the phantom jets showed up with their loads of napalm bombs. A few of them were caught in a fiery death before they could escape but most of them managed to melt safely back into the jungle.

The Cav lost five tracks and one Sheridan Tank to the heavy enemy RPG fire. Twelve men were killed in action and twenty three wounded. Two of the Lieutenants were killed and the third was seriously wounded which left Sergeant Mac officially in charge.

The Cav considered itself lucky. They must have been outnumbered twenty to one. One hundred and sixty three enemy bodies were counted. Twenty eight of them were inside the Cav's perimeter wire or at least what was left of it. Three enemy bodies were found in the mortar pit crushed to death by Sergeant Macs tank. Six more bodies were dug out from the caved in entrance to the tunnel. One man volunteered to go in and search the tunnel. He tied a rope around his waist and crawled in with a flashlight and a forty five caliber pistol. He came back half an hour later and reported a maze of interconnected tunnels. He said it would take days to explore them all.

Sergeant Mac got orders from higher up to change his position. He was to place half his tracks on either side of the old runway so they could act as security for two C-130s that were to arrive at twelve hundred hours.

"So that's why they wanted us here." Sergeant Mac said to FO.

"You've got to be kidding!" Said FO. "What the fuck would they want to land a couple C-130s on this god forsaken hill for."

"I don't know," said Sergeant Mac "and to tell you the truth I don't think I want to know."

Sergeant Mac told his men over the radio to change their position. "We've got to get away from these burning tracks before that cooking live ammo kills somebody." The tracks were burning so hot they were melting and the ammunition was going off throwing bullets, brass casings, hand grenades and anything else in every direction. The men loaded up the tracks while the cooking ammo sent shrapnel whizzing through the air all around them. The rounds didn't have as much force as ones fired through a weapon but they could still kill someone. The shrapnel could be heard bouncing off the tracks as the men worked. Everyone was wearing their flack jackets and steel pots. Many a man thanked his lucky stars as he felt a piece of hot shrapnel bounce off him. There were also a few screams as pieces hit flesh, most of them didn't break the skin but they stung like mad and raised quite a welt. The few rounds that did break the skin were extremely painful for they would burrow into the flesh and cook it with a sizzling sound from the hot metal.

Some of the wounded had to be loaded onto tracks or carried by stretcher to the new position. It was a lot of work but it had to be done because the choppers couldn't land close to the burning tracks.

As the Cav was setting up in their new position the medevac helicopters appeared on the horizon lead by several Cobra gunships. The gunships came in first circling the Cav's perimeter and opening up on suspected enemy positions with their mini-guns.

This time they were lucky. They managed to get all the wounded out without incident. Cyrano, Doc and the remaining two medics had been working their asses off and were quite relieved to watch the medevacs finally disappear over the horizon.

Chapter 22
Big LZ

"We've got to have resupply choppers in here ASAP." Sergeant Mac was on the horn talking to Quang Tri TOC. Control of their operation had been switched from Dong Ha to a higher higher at the Quang Tri Tactical Operations Center bunker.

Quang Tri TOC was a massive underground bunker complex complete with meeting rooms and a high ranking officers mess. It was said that the food there was better than most expensive New York restaurants. Steak and lobster was not an uncommon offering on their menu.

"Don't worry about a thing," Quang Tri TOC answered back to Sergeant Mac, "this operation has top priority over everything in Northern I Corp. Your supply choppers are on their way and should arrive at your position in ten mikes."

Doc and Cyrano were laying out in the early morning sun on stretchers trying to catch some shut eye before the midday heat would make it impossible. They were in the sun because their skin was bothering them, everybody's skin was bothering them, they called it jungle rot. It came from being in a foreign country and not being able to take a bath. That was the official word anyway. Some of the Doctors though said it was caused by the spraying being done to defoliate the land and take the enemy's hiding places away. Whatever the true cause was, the sun seemed to help. They were both just starting to nod off when the sound of choppers coming in woke them up. The birds came in fast and dropped off their load in a hurry while their escort Cobras circled the hilltop firing their mini-guns to keep the enemy's heads down once again. And once again they were lucky, no enemy fire.

Sergeant Mac was not happy though. He was on the horn once again. "You only gave us half the ammo we need!"

"Sorry 'bout that," answered back Quang Tri TOC, "but they were all the choppers we could get free for your drop. Don't worry about a thing though, your orders are to head back for Dong Ha this afternoon. You will be in a secured area before dark."

"That'll work just fine if we don't run into any ambushes on the way but the chances of that happening are slim and none. And another thing, what happened to the reason we were sent here in the first place?"

"There's been a change of orders from higher higher. The important thing now is to protect those C-130s when they come in, and as far as your trip back down Highway 9 goes you'll have air cover the whole way. Quang Tri TOC out."

"Damn it, I hate having to depend on those REMFs for our survival!" Sergeant Mac said to FO who was sitting next to him on top their Sheridan tank.

"I hear ya," said FO "but think about it man, that's what my whole job consists of."

There were two men on guard on each track but the majority of the Cav was trying to make up for the sleep they'd missed last night, and the many nights before. The sound of the first C-130 coming in woke everybody. They weren't used to hearing C-130s land in the field and the loud noise was disorienting to them at first.

"Mount up and man your guns." Sergeant Mac yelled out. The cry was echoed by other sergeants all around the Cav Troop's perimeter. Ten Cobra gunships appeared out of nowhere and began circling the hill called Khe Sanh.

As the Cobras swept the surrounding jungle with their mini-guns a huge roar came from the C-130 as it reversed its engines to land on what was left of the short hilltop runway. The huge transport plane gently touched down on the old runway slowly bouncing across its rough surface and finally lumbering to a stop inside the Cav Troop's perimeter. The dust was just beginning to settle when three mortar rounds landed in front of the giant bird showering the tracks closest to the runway with shrapnel. A terrifying scream of "medic" was yelled. Doc, Cyrano and the other two remaining medics ran as fast as they could toward the injured men as three more mortars landed behind the vulnerable grounded bird. One of the rounds made a direct hit on Doc and Cyrano's track killing instantly the driver and one other man who was sitting on top.

By this time three of the Cobras had found the enemy mortar on a nearby hill and were pelting it with mini-gun fire and rockets. One of them was hit by anti-aircraft machine gun fire. It burst into flames and crashed to the ground in pieces, there were no survivors. Two of the other Cobras peeled off from Khe Sanh and attacked the small hill. The mortar tube had already been knocked out and in a matter of seconds the four Cobras working together silenced the fifty caliber machine gun. One of the Cobras had sustained damage and had to return to Quang Tri.

By the time the second C-130 appeared, coming from the southeast, the Cobras had taken care of the hill and all eight of them were back circling Khe Sanh. The second C-130 landed a little rough, bounced along the runway and came to halt just behind the first one. It then turned around so they were tail to tail and both planes slowly lowered their huge hydraulic hatches.

Although both planes were C-130s, their similarities went no further. The plane that came in from the west looked like it was from some sort of civilian airline. It had no military insignia, as a matter of fact it had no markings at all. The whole plane had just that silvery metallic look of an unpainted airplane.

The second plane had camouflage paint in different colored patterns unlike most of the military planes, which were just plain olive drab. It also had a very distinctive marking on it, along side The South Vietnam red and yellow flag it read ARVN, Army of the Republic of Vietnam.

Chapter 23
No Honeymoon

Back at the Ranch, earlier that morning while the Cav was still fighting for its survival and the ownership of Khe Sanh, Fingers and The Monkey Man had been making the final preparations for their next mission. Six troop-carrying Huey helicopters were sitting on the ground warming up their engines. Fifty Meo, or as they preferred to be called; Hmong soldiers, waited nearby.

"Those Air America boys will never believe this one" said Fingers.

"Yea, it'll be quite a caper if we can pull it off" said The Monkey Man.

"Just what I've always wanted," said Fingers, "my very own tank!"

"Come on," said The Monkey Man, "they're for the Hmong Tribe."

"Hey, don't worry, I'll let 'em *use* it once in a while."

"All right men let's go, mount up." The Monkey Man yelled above the roar of the chopper engines. Six Green Berets all got into The Monkey Man's black chopper while the Hmong Tribesmen clamored aboard the five other choppers. They took off quickly heading to the east in the direction of Khe Sanh.

When they got close they kept to the north staying well out sight from any enemy troops who were in the vicinity of Khe Sanh. One by one the Hmong choppers found separate LZs to the north of Highway 9, once again making sure to keep a good distance from the highway where concentrations of NVA soldiers were believed to be.

When the Hmong left their choppers they stayed in small groups spreading out along the most dangerous part of Highway 9 close to Khe Sanh. This section of Highway 9 was well known to any GI who ever worked in the area. They called it ambush alley. The Hmong mission was to ambush the ambushers.

The Monkey Man's chopper continued on to the east until it reached Mai Loc, Hoang and Tray's village. Tray, Hoang and his two friends had easily survived the mountain top attack by hiding in a cave. The chopper coming in brought a great deal of excitement and apprehension to the sleepy little village.

Although it was late morning most of the adults were still asleep. They were recovering from last night's celebration, Hoang and Tray's wedding party. The chopper landing woke up most of the village but because of bad experiences with some Americans in the past the villagers stayed in their hootches. The young children though did not share their parents apprehensions, or their hangovers from the previous night. They all ran out to greet the helicopter with excited visions of chocolate bars and C-ration treats. Fingers was always prepared for such occasions. He stood like a giant among the screaming little kids holding a sandbag full of treats high over his head, and like some sort of weird Santa Claus rained chocolate bars down on the screaming mass.

Even with a hangover the sound of an incoming chopper woke Hoang instantly. After many years fighting with the VC that reflex had been ingrained into his consciousness for his very survival. He was disoriented at first, waking up in a village with a roof over his head. His first instinct was to run for his life. Tray woke up with him and seeing the confusion on his face threw her arms around him and calmed him down. Slowly they began gathering Hoang's gear together, extremely disappointed in the fact that his leave had been cut short.

The Monkey Man didn't bother to look for Hoang. He waited at the chopper with the rest of the men watching Fingers play Santa Claus. Finally Hoang came running to the chopper looking a little disheveled but none the less ready to go. "Sorry about cutting your leave short," said The Monkey Man, "but I'm afraid we've got another emergency."

Tray watched the chopper lift off and disappear over the mountains to the west. She was worried about Hoang's safety. She hated Hoang's new job already but she realized that because of his young age he had no choice in the matter. If he wasn't fighting with the Americans, either the ARVNs or the VC would force him to fight for their armies. She figured he was probably safer with Fingers and The Monkey Man. They at least seemed to know what they were doing and they paid a lot better.

Chapter 24
Friendly Fire

At Khe Sanh, Cyrano was freaking out. He was running towards the burning Medical Track yelling "My jeep, my jeep!"

Sergeant Mac grabbed him by the collar of his shirt like he was grabbing a puppy by the nap of the neck and yelled "What the hell is wrong with you son? There's an injured man on the ground next to your track and you're worried about your god damn jeep? Go help that man, I'll take care of your jeep!" Cyrano ran to the injured man feeling pretty stupid. The sergeant was right but Cyrano figured he had close to one million dollars worth of heroin in the back of that jeep.

The front end of the track was burning. The engine was already engulfed in flames but Sergeant Mac managed to disconnect the tow bar from the jeep before the track started exploding.

Sergeant Mac had known Cyrano for some time and knew it wasn't like him to ignore an injured soldier. He figured there had to be something mighty valuable in that jeep and he had a good idea of what it might be. This idea was heightened by the fact that Sergeant Mac knew Cyrano had just come back from Laos.

Sergeant Mac was a big man and he had no trouble pushing the little jeep a good distance from the burning track. When he'd got it a safe distance away he began a thorough search of everything in the jeep. The first thing he found was a large bag of marijuana. He expected to find that but it wasn't what he was looking for. Sergeant Mac didn't care much for pot but he also considered himself to be a reasonable man, unlike a lot of the officers. He knew a lot of the men smoked, there just wasn't much he could do about it. He figured if the men had to get high on something he'd rather it be weed than alcohol, at least that way they could still shoot straight and they didn't make as much noise as a drunk.

Sergeant Mac knew his men were under a great deal of pressure and he couldn't blame them for using something to help them relax. The Army used Ritalin for what it called battle fatigue. "Ha", thought Sergeant Mac, "everybody out here was tired of the battle but that Ritalin stuff the Army used turned his men into passive zombies, it worked better than alcohol but not much".

After a little more searching Sergeant Mac finally found what he was looking for, white powder. China White heroin, or smack as the men called it. He brought it to where Cyrano was still working on the injured man and waited until he had finished. Then Sergeant Mac held the million dollar bag before Cyrano and yelled "Cyrano you stupid fucking asshole, you see this? I should have you thrown in the Long Bin jail. They'll keep you there for the duration of this war and if you survive they'll give you a dishonorable discharge so you'd never be able to get a decent job. Instead I'm going to do you a favor."

"No, that's a million..." Cyrano began to protest but it was to late. Sergeant Mac threw the sack of heroin into the burning track and walked away without looking back. Cyrano cringed and watched in disbelief.

The sound of a chopper suddenly appeared out of nowhere and by the time the men looked around it was hovering a few feet off the ground alongside the huge C-130 transport planes.

Fingers and The Monkey Man were the first two out. They directed the rest of their men to form a circle around the rear loading platforms of the two big planes which were facing back to back. The Green Beret soldiers formed their small circle with their weapons at the ready facing out away from the C-130s and towards the Cav in their large circle around the planes.

The men of the Cav, who were sitting on their tracks watching this little piece of choreography, started to grumble as soon as they realized the Green Berets were there to protect the cargo from the Cav who had been fighting for their lives all night.

The grumbling started to get louder and was punctuated by the metallic clanking of the bolts of M16 rifles as they chambered a round and clicked their safety switches to the off position. The Green Berets stood their ground without flinching.

"Hey now, you guys wouldn't shoot a fellow American would ya?" Yelled The Monkey Man.

"Hold your fire for a few minutes men while I find out what these green beanies are up to," hollered Sergeant Mac as he slowly climbed down from his tank and ambled over to The Monkey Man.

"Ah come on Sarge, I always wanted to get me one a' them fancy French berets" yelled a voice from one of the Cav Troopers.

"Well Mister Monkey Fingers!" Said Sergeant Mac as he shook The Monkey Man's hand with a bone crunching grip. "We meet again. I'd like to thank you for your help at the Rock Pile, but hey, what the hell do you think you're doing here?"

"Our orders are to protect this shipment of goods for the Saigon government."

"You don't really believe you can take on the Cav all by yourselves do ya?" Said Sergeant Mac.

"We've got air support if we need it." Said The Monkey Man. "You might be able to kill us but if you did you'd be signing your own death warrants. The fact is Sergeant whether you realize it or not, you're in big trouble here. We know you're short on ammo and without our help you'll never make it out of here alive."

"Goddammit," said Sergeant Mac, "I've had a bad feeling about this Khe Sanh operation all along. I know damn well higher higher's been feeding us lies. This is one of those CIA spook operations isn't it?"

The Monkey Man just smiled and didn't say a word.

"Shit," said Sergeant Mac "those CIA assholes don't care who lives or dies so long as they turn a profit."

"Calm down now Sergeant. You've got to understand their looking at the big picture. They know what they're doing and as long as you cooperate we'll get you and your men out of here. Agreed Sergeant Mac?"

"Shit," said the Sergeant, "I don't really have any choice do I!" With that Sergeant Mac turned to his troops and yelled "Men we're going to be working with these fellow Americans for a while so keep your weapons pointed in the other direction towards the enemy you're supposed to be guarding against. Shit they could have snuck up on us and you men wouldn't have even noticed." The men grumbled a bit more but most of them locked their weapons while at least one man per track took the guard position at the fifty cal facing away from the C-130s.

"Sergeant" said The Monkey Man, "we've already got ground troops deployed along route nine and air support on the way so we'd like to make a little deal with you."

As Sergeant Mac and The Monkey Man continued their conversation the crew of the Air America C-130 began unloading its cargo while the crew of the ARVN plane loaded it back into theirs.

Everything seemed to be going smoothly until Sergeant Mac bellowed out "Two tanks!" He yelled so loud that everybody stopped what they were doing and stared at him.   Unshaken, The Monkey Man put one arm around the big shoulders of Sergeant Mac and while gesturing with the other he calmly continued the conversation.

Fingers, disturbed by the slow down in the loading yelled out "let's move it people this isn't a social gathering."

The loaders went back to their work at a faster pace than before. One of them an ARVN soldier moved so fast that he tripped over the ramp of his plane and off onto the ground landing on top of his package. It split open and a white powder poured out of it onto the ground. A loud gasp came up from all the men watching and then whispered words of "smack", "china white" and "jeese it's heroin!"

The Air Force Colonel who had been forced to fly the Air America plane because of a shortage of Air America pilots walked over to the spot where the soldier had fallen. He was dressed in a flight suit without any insignia or rank and he looked extremely angry. The Colonel wore his anger like a General wears his stars. It was obvious he was in charge. When he got to the fallen man he was met by an ARVN General who looked at him curiously wondering why he should be so angry over such a small mistake.

The Colonel bent down to the open bag, stuck a finger into the white powder, brought it to his mouth and tasted it. The anger on his face instantly doubled. He grabbed the confused ARVN General and yelled, "You goddamn asshole. We send you our boys to protect your country and you sell them heroin for your own personal gain."

This didn't explain what the Colonel was doing flying the heroin to him in the first place but since the ARVN General didn't understand English it made no difference to him anyway.

In his anger the Colonel pushed him face first into the split open bag of heroin and held him there kicking and gurgling until he started to turn blue. One of the unfortunate General's men then became so agitated that he shot and killed the American Air Force Colonel. This was quickly followed by one of the Green Berets shooting the ARVN soldier. When the Green Beret was shot by another ARVN soldier though, all hell broke lose. The Cav opened up! At first it was just with their M16s but when the ARVNs fired back the Cav turned its tracks around and opened up with its fifty and sixty caliber machine guns. In less than one minute the entire crew of the ARVN C-130 were dead. Sergeant Mac well knew when the Cav opens up its hard to get them to stop. By the time the ARVN aircraft burst into flames Sergeant Mac had already been hollering at the top of his lungs "cease fire!" For quite some time.

When the firing finally stopped Doc and Cyrano went to work on the two men from the Cav who had been nicked by the ARVNs, no one from the Cav had been killed. A medevac was called by an RTO who was careful not to let on to what had just happened. The Green Berets had been lucky to suffer only the loss of one man. They had hit the dirt firing before the Cav opened up and when it was over they helped the crew of the Air America C-130 carry the body of the dead Colonel back aboard.

Sergeant Mac was yelling at his troops once more about the importance of fire discipline and bemoaning the fact that they had just wasted half of their remaining ammunition. By the time Sergeant Mac got back to his conversation with The Monkey Man he had gone through a sudden transformation in his willingness to give up two of his tanks. "Goddamn," said Sergeant Mac, "we're all in big trouble now! When higher higher finds out what happened here they're gonna hang our asses. And I seriously doubt if they'll send us another resupply chopper."

"Yea" said Fingers as he watched the ARVN C-130 burn. "There goes our next promotion."

"Don't worry Sergeant Mac," said The Monkey Man, "like I said before, we'll get your troops out'a here. Our ground troops are already in position along route nine and our air support is on the way."

"I think we'll need everything you've got." Said Sergeant Mac. "I'm gonna try one more time to get some ammo resupply."

As Sergeant Mac headed off to his tank the Air America C-130 took off from Khe Sanh with a deafening roar. As it neared the end of the runway several enemy mortars hit the ground nearby sending plumes of dirt and shrapnel into the air. The C-130 having avoided the near misses lifted into the air and began a steep climb headed back to Laos.

The Cobra gunship which had been circling the area finally left rather confused wondering why they'd even bothered to show up.

As a lone medevac helicopter came in to take the dead and wounded away Sergeant Mac was back on the horn trying to talk higher higher into sending him another load of ammunition, he wasn't having much luck. "Sergeant Mac what the hell is going on up there? I just got a report from some helicopter pilots that you guys opened up on the ARVNs."

"They opened up on the Green Berets first" said Sergeant Mac, "and what's more they were smuggling heroin."

"That's neither here nor there Sergeant Mac, it doesn't change what your men did. You realize this could be court-martial material? Hell of a war Sergeant, I'll do what I can to get you some ammo but I can't make any guarantees. I'm afraid I don't have the authority to make the final decision. I'll try to convince them. Shit Sergeant I wish I was out there with you guys. I hate sittin' on this goddamn radio."

"Thank you sir, I understand what you're sayin' but without that ammo we may never make it out of here. Right now I don't care about any court-martial, I just want to get these boys out of here alive!"

"I understand Sergeant and I'll do everything I can. Quebec Tango out!"

Sergeant Mac cursed at the hand set of his radio after the officer on duty at Quang Tri TOC signed off. Then he smashed it against the turret of his tank, it made him feel better, but not much.

Doc and Cyrano had just finished loading the dead and wounded onto the chopper when the mortars started coming in again. Doc noticed the fear on the chopper crew's faces as they lifted off, it almost made him feel glad to be on the ground. As they ran to a hole for cover they could hear the antiaircraft fire starting up again from a nearby mountain top. As they reached the hole they heard an explosion and looked up just in time to see the medevac burst into flames. Some of the men inside actually jumped out of the burning inferno and fell flailing and screaming to their deaths. Most of the men who witnessed the sight were forced to look away in horror.

"Just tryin' to fly" said Cyrano.

Doc shook his head and sighed "damn."

The mortars kept coming in and the men hunkered down where they could find even the illusion of cover, some into their tracks or any depression in the ground they could find.

The mortars were still falling when Quang Tri TOC came back on the radio. Sergeant Mac had to scrounge through his tank for another hand set before he could answer back. When he did he got a final answer about ammo resupply. "Sergeant Mac we've lost contact with your medevac and assume they went down."

"I'm afraid that's an affirmative" said Sergeant Mac. "Then you realize it's too dangerous to send a resupply chopper in there Sergeant. Your only hope is to get the hell out of there as fast as you can."

"I understand" said Sergeant Mac.

"Good luck!"

"Thank you sir, we'll need it. Bravo Troop out."

Sergeant Mac got on the horn to his men and gave the order. "Mount up men we're movin' out." The men on the ground were reluctant to move, for the most part they had found fairly safe spots by now, many of them had gone back to the same holes they had been fighting in the night before. The constant mortar barrage was keeping their heads down. The men in the tracks though, did not feel nearly so secure. Even though their ammunition was low they were still sitting on top a lot of 50 and 60 rounds not to mention all the claymores and hand grenades. A direct hit by a mortar round in the right spot would send them high into the sky.

They started their engines and began forming up single file. This got the men on the grounds attention right away as they ran to the tracks one unfortunate soul received a direct hit from an incoming mortar. Somebody yelled medic but when Doc ran out to investigate he could not find enough left of the man to bother with, not even his dog tags. Doc didn't even know who the man had been. He just hoped someone knew so he wouldn't be listed as missing in action.

The Green Berets spread out, each of them hopped aboard a separate track or tank. The Monkey Man climbed onto Sergeant Macs tank, Fingers and Hoang hopped into the jeep with Doc and Cyrano.

The mortars kept coming in and followed the line of tracks as they headed out back to Highway 9. Fortunately they were not accurately aimed and weren't scoring any lucky hits. Still the white hot metal being thrown out by them as shrapnel was causing a number of wounds among the men, some of them serious, and men were dying. Their buddies aboard their tracks were doing what they could to help them. Stopping the bleeding and wrapping the wounds with field dressings but there wasn't time now to stop and let the medics help them. They had to move out of this place as fast as they could or they would never move anywhere again.

Chapter 25
Blast From The Past

Sergeant Mac, sitting next to The Monkey Man on his Sheridan tank, turned to him and said, "If you can really get my men out of here I'll gladly give you all the tanks we've got left, and from the looks of things right now that'll be zero."

"Not to worry Sergeant Mac all we need is two of them. We'll get ya outa' here!"

The battered line of tanks and Armored Personnel Carriers made its way as fast as it could down the winding road from the hill of Khe Sanh onto Highway 9 and headed east through ambush alley to its hoped for destination of Dong Ha. Not many of the men really believed they would make it that far.

The Monkey Man told Sergeant Mac not to let his men open up on anything along the road unless it was first OK'd by him or one of his men on the other tracks. "We've got friendlies working all the way down Highway 9. They're scouting out ambushes and marking mines for us. I don't know if there's enough of them to find all the enemy sights but I'm willing to bet they'll find most of them, they're good soldiers."

The Cav continued on traveling at top speed and with the one remaining empty track in the lead. The men of the Cav trusted the Green Berets a little but they didn't know or trust the Hmong at all. The Green Berets realized that and knew they would have a tough time controlling their heavy trigger fingers. Their first encounter with the Hmong though would change their minds.

The driver of the lead track was the first to notice the small arms fire. He could see tracer rounds arcing through the air in front of him but he couldn't see where they were coming from because of a rise in the road before him. The driver cautiously slowed down setting off a chain reaction that resulted in all of the tracks bunching together. Sergeant Mac was on the horn right away screaming at the lead track to speed up, and at the rest of the tracks to maintain their distances. The lead track finally came flying over the rise in the road onto the awesome sight of a fire fight in progress. Red tracers were coming from the tree line on the left and green tracers from the tree line on the right.

The Monkey Man gave Sergeant Mac permission to fire into the tree line on the right. Sergeant Mac wasted no time letting his men know and in a matter of seconds the tree line on the right exploded with incoming fifty and sixty caliber machine gun fire.

The tracks kept firing as they moved, finally coming to a stop between the NVA and the Hmong. The fire was so intense from the Cav that the NVA didn't dare raise their heads to fire an RPG.

The Monkey Man signaled the Hmong to come to the tracks. They came out of the tree line at a dead run and clamored aboard the tracks.

As the tracks quickly accelerated to get away from the ambush site a few of the tracks were forced to stop firing, they had run out of ammo! Some brave NVA soldiers took advantage of the situation to open up with their RPGs. The men of the Cav instinctively ducked down on top of their tracks as the terrifying whoosh of the RPGs flew by them. Most of them missed or glanced harmlessly off the tanks armor. One though scored a direct hit on a track. Screams from the men were heard as the track burst into flames.

The tracks behind stopped to pick up the survivors and because of this Sergeant Mac was forced to stop the rest of the Troop to give them supporting fire. More tracks began running out of ammunition and the NVA started firing volleys of RPGs. Two more tracks were quickly hit and knocked out of action. More tracks were running out of ammo! Sergeant Mac looked to The Monkey Man in despair and said "Mister Monkey Fingers, we're in deep shit!" The Monkey Man was standing up on the tank looking to the rear at the horizon. He didn't say a word. Sergeant Mac followed his gaze and turned around. What he saw brought him back almost twenty years to when he was a young private in Korea, a blast from the past! Prop driven fighter planes, A-1 Sky raiders. The Monkey Man got on his radio to direct their fire.

The NVA were caught completely off guard, the noise of the machine gun fire blocked out the sound of the prop driven planes as they dove in low on their target. When the Sky raiders came within range of their target they opened up with machine guns and dropped their heavy loads of High Explosive bombs. The enemy was wiped out in a matter of seconds by the low, slow flying, and extremely accurate aircraft.

The men of the Cav, who just a few short seconds ago had thought they were doomed to die on the infamous Yellow Brick Road, were now wildly cheering on their unlikely looking saviors. "Holy shit!" Said Cyrano to Doc and Fingers. "When I saw those old planes sitting on the ground at the Ranch and Long Tieng I never would have believed that in a few days they would be saving my life. Shit, I didn't even believe they could still fly!"

Sergeant Mac stood up in the turret of his tank and bellowed out "Forward haooo!" The Cav moved out at top speed, most of them were out of ammo but for the first time in quite a while they actually believed they had a good chance of making it back to Dong Ha alive.

Ten A-1 Sky raiders came up from behind them, their huge internal combustion engines blowing out blue black smoke behind them. They roared just over the heads of the Cav and rocked their wings in recognition as they past over while the Cav cheered them on.

Every so often the men would hear explosions far in front of them as they sped to the east down Highway 9. As they approached the area where the explosions had taken place the dust would still be settling down through the air and like some sort of a mirage the Hmong would be standing in the road barely visible through the fog of red dust. Their weapons at the ready staring intensely into the tree line waiting for their Green Beret friends to come and pick them up in those strange looking American elephants.

The Hmong of course had been told that the tanks were not really alive but sometimes they had a tough time believing it. As a matter of fact a lot of the Cav Troops also thought of their tracks as being alive. They were indeed a strange welding of man and machine. They even smelled alive with a combination of oil and diesel fuel mixed in with the blood, sweat and tears of their occupants.

As the Cav approached the waiting Hmong they would come to a halt and the Hmong would scramble up on top the tracks while the Sky raiders who had been circling up high would dive low to the tree lines on either side of the road looking for possible ambushes.

The Cav made good progress, they were moving as fast as they had coming in, but this time they were traveling with a great deal more safety. When the first group of fighter bombers began to run short of fuel a second group came flying in from the west. Moving fast and low to the ground they buzzed by the line of tracks and kept going to the east scouting out the Yellow Brick Road while the original Sky raiders turned around and flew by the Cav for the last time dipping their wings as the Cav waved them goodbye.

Chapter 26

A Company Job

After almost a week of nerve racking tension Doc and Cyrano were for the first time beginning to relax a little. They were beginning to feel that they just might make it back to Dong Ha from their R and R, and what an R and R it was. There would be some stories to be told. Many of which no one would believe.

Fingers turned to Doc and said "Quite a week, uh?"

"Yea," said Doc, "but to tell you the truth I'm not even sure if I believe half of what I think happened."

"Well," said Fingers, "you guys have been through a lot of shit in a short amount of time. Life threatening shit. You've seen a lot of people die and you knew it could just as well have been you. You haven't had more than a few hours sleep a night for the whole time, sometimes no sleep at all.

"Yea," said Cyrano, "but to tell you the truth I don't even feel tired."

"Yea I know" said Fingers, "I've been through it many times myself. You guys are wired! You've had so much adrenaline pumpin' through your system for so long that you're on a sort of permanent high. Eventually it will wear off but it'll take time. Right now you don't realize it but your perceptions of reality are distorted. Your mind can play tricks on you. There's a tendency for you to misinterpret things you see. They become more grandiose. You've seen a lot of ugly things that your mind doesn't really want to except. So it doesn't, and your memory of what really happened can become distorted. Instead of remembering all the blood and guts and chunks of faces and brains you tend to remember things that are a little easier for your mind to except. Things that are more interesting and exciting. Things that you want to think and talk about, curious stuff."

"Yea," said Cyrano, "curiouser and curiouser!"

"You know," said Doc, "I could have swore I saw old Tyrannosaurus Rex when we were flying into Laos. And then there was that strange incident with the Shaman from the old tribe, well come to think of it that whole ancient tribe trip was just a little too much to believe. I see your point Fingers. I'm not too sure of just exactly what was real and what wasn't."

"That's just what I mean," said Fingers, "I've had some of those experiences myself. Not to mention some of the stories I've heard. T-Rex is a pretty common one along with UFOs, and that old tribe we ran into, I've heard stories about them before too. Believe it or not some of the stories I've heard make our run in with them look down right tame. Maybe some of the stories are true, I don't really know."

"What I'm getting to here though is something you've got to watch out for." Fingers continued, "After living like this for a while all the excitement starts to get to ya in a strange sort of way. You actually get used to it. The adrenaline rush you get from combat becomes a normal state for ya and you almost start looking forward to it. It's like your body becomes addicted to that rush of adrenaline you get everyday being out here. Then when your tour is up and they send you home you end up going through a sort of withdrawal from all the excitement you've become used to. It makes you want to do crazy things when you get home, and if you don't you'll become depressed. Sort of a no-win situation if you're not careful. That's why so many combat veterans end up signing up for second and third tours. It becomes a way of life, I know. This is almost the end of my third tour."

"So what are you going to do when they send you home this time?" asked Doc, "I mean they only let you serve three tours over here."

"Well," said Fingers, "me and The Monkey Man have been talkin' to some of the CIA boys and they've offered us a job working for Air America. As a matter of fact that's the connection we used to get the C-130s and the Sky raiders to work with us. They've offered us jobs that actually pay good money, not like this Army bullshit we've been putting up with all these years. Makes me wonder why we stayed in so long. I tell ya, me and The Monkey Man are gonna be rich, and benefits, life and health insurance, the whole nine yards!"

"Sounds good for ya" said Doc. "Ever since I met you guys I've thought you were too smart to stay in the Army. I tell ya though Fingers, there's somethin' that's been buggin' me for a couple months now and I think if anybody knows the answer to this question it's you."

"I think I know what your question is," said Fingers, "I've seen it in your eyes for some time now. You want to know why we're here, fightin' this war. I'm afraid I can't really answer that question for ya. I mean fightin' communism is a good thing, people need to be free and freedom is something you have to fight for, but I don't think that's the reason we're here. I mean the South Vietnamese people are good people but their government is corrupt as hell, like that C-130 with the heroin. I don't think their government is really worth fighting for. It's the common folk we're fightin' for, but the irony of it all is that they're the ones who are being hurt the most by wars. That's why I decided to join Special Forces after my first tour. I saw how fucked up this war was and figured if we were gonna be here anyway at least I'd be able to help the people who need it and not the fat cats in Saigon. The small Tribes and villages, they're the ones I'm fighting for and they do need our help. But the question you're asking really goes far beyond all of that. It's a matter of evolution. The only reason the human race has survived as long as it has is because of our aggressive nature. The fact that we're good fighters has kept us alive."

"I don't know if I can buy that" said Doc. "It may have been true once, but with our modern weapons I think we are eventually going to destroy ourselves through war. Times have changed, and if the human race doesn't evolve into a peaceful race it will destroy itself."

"That sounds right to me" said Fingers. "In the future I think we *might* evolve into a peaceful race but just look around you man, look at how primitive these people are. I mean most of these tribes have just stepped out of the stone age. You still think the way people do back in the world. You've got to realize that most of the people on this earth don't live like we do back in the states. These people are fighting for their very survival, and without our help I'm afraid it's gonna be hard."

Hoang had been listening quietly and decided it was his time to speak up for his people. "It's true," he said, "The South Vietnamese, Hmong, the Montagnards do not stand much chance against North Vietnamese without American help. Part of reason is they don't want to fight against common enemy. They consider themselves separate countries, not friendly with each other. It is true that South Vietnamese government is corrupt so many of their people fight against them as VC."

"But", he continued, "you must understand what caused these problems in first place. Our people have been fighting to govern themselves for many generations. We grow up with war, like our fathers before us. We fought the Chinese and the Mongols and they occupied us, but we defeated them. We were the only country to defeat Genghis Khan. We were occupied by the French and Japanese. It took hundreds of years to defeat the French who were supported by the Americans, but we did. And now you Americans are here. You say you help us win our freedom from the Communists in the north but the government you support is nothing but your puppets. They are corrupt and do not care about the Vietnamese people."

"Hoang," said Fingers, "The Monkey Man told me he thought you'd been working with the VC for awhile, as a matter of fact that's part of the reason he decided to hire you. He figured you knew what was going on around here."

"Yea, that's right," said Doc, "you were with that group that attacked our platoon a few weeks back. We got two of them but one guy got away. We were right next to your home village of Mai Loc and that's where Tray is from too. As a matter of fact when we picked up Tray at Quang Tri, I thought I recognized her from some place. Then it came to me. She was the woman we picked up as a VC sympathizer in Mai Loc the morning after we'd been attacked. You got away though and hid out with some other VC in the mountains near the Rock Pile. I know that for a fact because we went out on a foot patrol through some rugged terrain and found your camp. We caught you by surprise. I guess you didn't expect the Cav to be sending out foot patrols. Your guards were alert though and you managed to escape, but you had to leave everything but your personal weapons behind. Well, we went through your stuff and I found this." Doc pulled a picture of Tray out of his pocket and handed it to Hoang. "I guess this is yours Hoang. It's got your name on the back, looks like a little love note from Tray. I went through the souvenirs in my fifty can the other day and when I saw this I figured I should give it back to ya."

"Yes this is my picture," said Hoang, "thank you for returning it. I feel bad now about the booby trap we set for you that day. I watched it go off from a distance and saw one of your men die. But I know that if you had the chance you would have killed all of us. So much killing. I sometimes feel that it will never end, but Doc we are on the same side. We both fight for the people, for the tribes and the small villages like my home, Mai Loc. I just hope that the fighting will be over and we can go on with our lives."

"I hear ya" said Fingers, "but us Americans, we're lucky. When our tour is up we can go home and at least try to forget this ever happened."

"I don't think I'll ever forget this" said Doc.

"Yea" said Fingers. "maybe that's why I'm still here."

Their conversation was interrupted by the roar of two C-130 airplanes which flew over their column at tree top level and landed on the road in front of them.

The Cav pulled into a circle around the two C-130s their guns pointed out to the flat ground around them. To the northwest were the gently rolling foot hills that quickly turned into the rocky towering peaks of the Rock Pile and then into the mountain ranges of Laos. They were in a relatively secure position now, still on Highway 9 but close to Highway 1 the main artery of Vietnam that ran up and down its coast along the South China Sea. Although the men sat at their machine guns it was only a show of force. They were almost out of ammunition and they all knew it. Despite this fact the men of the Cav felt safe. As a matter of fact this was the first time they'd felt safe since they left Dong Ha almost a week ago. It seemed like a lifetime ago, and for many of them it had been a lifetime.

The Cav had lost nearly seventy percent of their vehicles and twenty percent of their personnel. Most of them had died at Khe

Sanh, or on the Yellow Brick Road on the way there. They were still carrying many of their dead and wounded with them. The Cav was now in secure enough territory to call a medevac in. Doc, Cyrano and the one other remaining medic made the rounds to see how many men needed to be flown out. Some of the men who had been seriously wounded had died on the road out of Khe Sanh. That road seemed to be just plane unlucky. People died there even when they weren't being shot at.

    The medics checked all the wounded and the ones who were still alive were all in stable condition. Doc suggested calling in a medevac for them anyway. He figured there was no need to take any chances. But the men all refused to go. They'd been through a lot and figured they might as well finish the job since only the easy part was left. All they had to do was ride back into Dong Ha looking like heroes. They figured the lifers were trying to get rid of them with this mission and they wanted to prove to them that it couldn't be done. They couldn't wait to see the look in the colonels eyes when their rag tag band of shot up tracks paraded into the motor pool at Dong Ha. That Colonel was going to be scared for his life for the rest of his tour.

    The Green Berets had gathered around Sergeant Mac's Sheridan tank. There was a lot of laughing and joking going on. Fingers climbed up on the tank as Sergeant Mac started climbing down. They shook hands as they met and Sergeant Mac said "it's all yours son, you've earned it." Fingers climbed down into the drivers seat with a smile on his face and proceeded to drive his very own tank to the waiting C-130, up the ramp and into the cargo hold. He was quickly followed by another Green Beret driving the second tank into the other waiting C-130.

    The planes had kept their engines running and within sixty seconds both the tanks, all the Hmong tribesmen and the Green Berets were inside the planes. As the hydraulic rear doors of the giant C-130s began to close The Monkey Man stood at attention and saluted Sergeant Mac and the rest of his Cav Troop. Sergeant Mac stood ram rod straight and saluted back. The rest of the Cav followed suit although in a bit more of a relaxed manor. Only a few of them stood at attention but they all gave at least their own version of a salute. After all, The Monkey Man had saved their lives.

As the ramps slammed shut the engines of the giant birds roared to a deafening pitch and slowly at first they began to inch forward down the rough dirt road. Quickly they gained momentum, and in a time and distance which seemed impossible for such massive hulks loaded down with tanks, they were off the ground and gaining altitude. They banked hard to the left, and as the Cav watched the two C-130s climbed over the rocky hills of the Rock Pile and in a matter of minutes disappeared over the mountains of Laos.

Chapter 27
R And R

Doc and Cyrano had made their way to where Sergeant Mac was standing. Sergeant Mac bellowed out, "Now remember men, those two tanks were lost in action at Khe Sanh. I don't want to lose my retirement over this little deal."

"Don't worry about it." Yelled out one of the men. "Nobody'd believe this story anyway!"

"Hey Sarge," yelled Cyrano, "are we free to go yet? I mean after all ya know we're still on R and R."

"Yea, I guess so," said Sergeant Mac, "just one thing though. If I ever even hear about you tryin' to make money off heroin again I'll have you thrown in the Long Bin jail for the duration of this war."

"Not to worry" said Cyrano. "You've shown me the light. From now on I'm stickin' to my old ways for makin' a buck. Which reminds me Sarge, I just happen to know where you can buy a bran' new Sheridan tank for real cheap, you interested Sarge?"

"That does it Cyrano," said Sergeant Mac, "get the hell outa' here!"

"Come on Doc let's get movin' before he changes his mind."

Doc and Cyrano ran quickly to the jeep, jumped in and were off on their way back to Highway 1 as fast as the jeep would carry them.

As they cruised down Highway 1, Cyrano turned to Doc and asked "Did ya find the answer to your ten thousand dollar question?"

"You mean," said Doc, "what we're doin' here fighting this war?"

"Yea, that's the one" said Cyrano.

"To tell you the truth," said Doc, "I'm still not sure, but at least I've got a good idea. I think the reason we're here is not so much political as it is humanitarian. Guess we're here to protect the common people. The farmers, the tribes and the small villages. It's a noble cause."

"It is a noble cause," said Cyrano "but I don't think it's the reason our government sent us here."

"No, maybe not" said Doc. "But since we've helped them start this war I'm afraid they will need our help until it's won."

"Yea," said Cyrano, "now that we've committed them, we've got to finish the job. Whatever we do we can't just abandon them. They'd be slaughtered by the Communists."

"I don't know," said Doc, "I can't believe we would leave this place without at least some kind of a truce, maybe like the way Korea ended."

"I hope you're right," said Cyrano, "but you heard what Fingers and The Monkey Man said, and they know more about what's going on than most of our politicians do."

"Shit," said Doc, "if you're right I feel sorry for Hoang and Tray or for that matter for anyone that's worked with the Americans."

"There it is!" Said Cyrano as his beat up, bullet riddled jeep sped down Highway 1 headed for Dong Ha.

As they pulled into the gate the same guard was on duty that was there when they left. "Holy shit," said the guard as they slowed down to greet him, "you guys look like you've been through hell. You must have had one wild R and R. I've never seen any one come back lookin' as dragged out as you two."

"It's a long story." Said Cyrano as the guard waved them through.

"I tell ya," said Doc, "that definitely did it for me. I mean I've got a rear echelon job now and from now on that's where I'm stayin". In the rear with the beer. I don't know what I was thinking of by takin' off like that, and on my R and R too."

"Yea," said Cyrano "but you've got to admit, it was one hell of an experience."

"Yea," said Doc grabbing the empty opium pouch that was still around his neck "but I'm not sure I believe half of it."

"Come on," said Cyrano, "let's hit the club and celebrate the end of our journey."

They parked the beat up jeep outside the EM club and walked through the saloon style swinging doors. When they stepped up to the bar to buy a beer a familiar sound was heard, the bell rang once again and the bar tender yelled out "drinks on the house."

"Goddamn," yelled Doc as he threw his boonie hat on the floor and stomped on it, "I did it again!"

"Ya know," said Cyrano, "you're gonna go broke bein' a REMF."

As they finally tipped up their beers a news cast came on the AFVN (American Forces Vietnam Network) radio station which had been playing music in the background. The bar tender turned up the volume and everybody in the bar stopped their conversations to listen. The news caster said "A message from the President of the United States." The familiar voice of Richard Nixon came on. "The Vietnamization of the war has been going ahead as scheduled and with a great deal of success. Within a year the majority of our troops will be home and in two years I hope to have all of our troops out of Vietnam. I have the utmost confidence in the Army of the Republic of Vietnam and know they will be able to continue the control of their country that our fighting men have helped them achieve. I have promised them our continued financial support until they are able to at last defeat the Communist threat to the north. The war is going well now and it should not take long. The lives of our fighting men will not have been in vain."

THE END

CLOSING NOTE

On October seventh of two thousand and one, at just 52 years of age, David L. Johnson, died of complications from hepatitis. This cause of death is only too common in Vietnam era veterans, where he was a decorated combat medic.

Like too many who die as a result of conflict around the world he is remembered as others continue to ask "Why?".